ANNO
KLARKASH-TON

ANNO
KLARKASH-TON

Edited by GLYNN BARRASS &
FREDERICK J. MAYER

Introduction by Frederick J. Mayer

RAINFALL BOOKS

Published in 2017 by

Rainfall Books
22 Woodland Park, Calne, Wiltshire. SN11 0JX. UK.
www.rainfallsite.com

FIRST EDITION

1 2 3 4 5 6 7 8 9 10

Rainfall Records & Books
CLOUD 052

ISBN 978-0-9563991-4-4
Printed in the United Kingdom

CONTENTS

Cover art by Bruce Pennington
Illustrated by Steve Lines

Introduction Frederick J. Mayer

POETRY

INSPIRED BY CLARK ASHTON SMITH
by Michael Fantina

A WREATHE OF SMITHICS JUST FOR YOU, A POPPY CROWN
By Charles Lovecraft

FICTION

ARTWORK

NON-FICTION

INTRODUCTION
CLARK ASHTON SMITH/KLARKASH-TON
or "Smith, Zothique and Me"
Dedicated to Carol Jones Dorman

I have the privilege of writing this Introduction to Anno Klarkash-Ton, as well as being its co-editor with Glynn Owen Barrass (whose love and devotion brought this volume into being, not to mention, having had published his valued Clark Ashton Smith bibliography long before, which this publication is more than a mere updated version). Ironically, this also marks for me the latest in a long line of personal encounters with the sorcerous spirit of the high priest of Zothique Klarkash-Ton/Clark Ashton Smith.

Unlike many modern day Smith connoisseurs, I didn't have my awareness of Clark Ashton Smith raised via his friend H. P. Lovecraft (by the way, the moniker "Klarkash-Ton" was originally CAS' creation not Lovecraft's as is so often mistakenly thought). It was the other way around for me. In 1970, I was attending the California State University, Sacramento. On September 16th (my birthday no less), I was hanging about the University's Honors Center's lounge area (an adjunct to the special Honors program Department) where all sorts of books could be found, usually concerning the latest "in" philosophical concepts. And, there casually tossed upon the pale carpet was the Ballantine paperback *Zothique* with its sensuously blood red alluring George Barr cover with its enchanting Sorceress. After reading it for about an hour, I decided to borrow it from the Center (eventually "stealing" it, it wasn't that kind of honor place for me I guess). I still have that paperback as it was one of the few books I brought with me when I moved to South Korea. Sorcerer Klarkash-Ton, as Smith friend/scholar Donald Sydney-Fryer so aptly dubbed him, had cast his spell and I have been a devotee ever since then.

It seems I was fated to have Clark Ashton Smith's "spirit" in some form or another interact with my life evermore in a most literal way which has allowed me to learn more about Smith the man of flesh and blood. About a year after my literary discovery, I was the poetry editor for the campus magazine I.E. whose professorial overseer was journalism teacher/respected sculptor Hal Ruben. One night while working on the zine's layout, for some reason I now forget, CAS came up and Hal told me that he was an acquaintance of Clark. On various occasions afterward Ruben would ask me to his home in still rural Auburn, show me what was left of the Smith homestead and introduced me to folks who "knew" Smith. Hal would recount experiences he had involving Clark as examples of how the man was truly a stranger in a familiar land. One of my favorites is how one day he went to visit Smith and found the wordsmith extraordinaire on his cabin roof sunbathing with Carol (Dorman)...au natural!

During my graduate days (same university), I took a class in what was then called "New Journalism" from one William Dorman. From Hal, I discovered that I was learning writing from Clark Ashton Smith's step-son! I soon became friends with Bill and he shared stories of what it was like having CAS as a "father," including what Bill and his sister sometimes heard through the thin walls of their Pacific Grove home (ironic was this location as Smith enjoyed his spirits and he was now partially living in one of California's, then, few remaining "Dry" localities).

What I will say about childhood memories concerning two very caring grown-ups is that some pet names the adult couple had for each other were "Captain Nemo" and "Princess Yoni." What I was absorbing from my overall interactions among Smith intimates manifested in one of my most popular published poems "The Abominations of Yoni." Thanks Sorcerer Smith! And, to oft-whispered queries about a creative spirit generally considered a sardonically misanthropic wit and his amorous human real life activities, Clark Ashton Smith in every sense of the word was truly a "Poet."

By 1976, I had firmly established my radio drama program *Arkham Theatre*. The program was eventually nationally syndicated (thanks to the aid of Ray Bradbury) winning an award along the way. However, my proudest moment didn't involve any of my own scripts.

Arkham Theatre performed the one act play *The Dead Will Cuckold You*, "A drama in six scenes" by Clark Ashton Smith. It was Bradbury who brought it to my attention and favorably recommended that we perform/produce it. Ray had gotten me a copy of *In Memoriam: Clark Ashton Smith* (see Anno bibliography) which, among other items, included Smith's play. In Memoriam was where the play was first published and I believe we at Arkham Theatre were the first to perform it.

I had a minor role within Cuckold alongside the great speaking and talented Fritz Leiber, Jr. Fritz agreed to perform in it because of his respect for CAS and his works, but more importantly because he met Smith once in Auburn and this was Leiber's way of saying "Thank You" to such a charming and kind person. It was my way of showing my gratitude to someone whose particular story cycle opened up whole new worlds to me. You see, Smith set *The Dead Will Cuckold You* (written about 1950, year of my birth) in Zothique!

Ray Bradbury had written the Introduction to In Memoriam, but I believe something more important to be known about its contents is its "Pre-foreword", a poem by Lady Carolyn (Carol Dorman). Carol has too often been overlooked when it comes to the importance this lady had in Smith's life.

In the last full decade of Smith's life, the 1950's, he was in his late 50's and saw definite highs and lows. Always somewhat of frail health yet other times robust enough to work manual harvest labor as well as building his cabin's stone wall rock by rock, in the early fifties, Smith started experiencing his eventual series of crippling strokes. This period marked such accomplishments such as Smith, at age 56, teaching himself Spanish, making his first translation of Spanish works and writing some original Spanish pieces (some eventually published as *Donde Duermes, Eldorado? Y Otro Poemas)* while returning to painting. Not to mention, he writes one of his last stories (if not the last) "Morthylla" (appears in *Weird Tales*, May, 1953), probably just before Cuckold and also set in Zothique. Interestingly, in Smith's waning years, of all his story cycles, he chooses to give birth to creations set in the waning future continent of earth. Smith falls in love with Carol Jones Dorman (a bit of a Bohemian herself) and they get married on November 10th, 1954. In a very real way, it is because of Carol's entry into Smith's world that his body and soul gained periods of health while providing him a material muse that keeps him a creatively producing spirit here when his physical and mental self was at extremely low ebbs! I suffered a minor stroke during the process of bringing Anno to fruition so I am acutely aware of the debt owed to Ms. Dorman-Smith.

Mrs. Smith dedicated her Pre-foreword to "Clark Ashton Smith." Here, I am pleased to state that I dedicate the Introduction to Anno Klarkash-Ton to "Carol Jones Dorman" as but a small acknowledgement to an exceptional person and "beloved enchantress of Klarkash-Ton."

My life continues with more wondrous and unsought out Klarkash-Tonian encounters and I appreciate the reader's indulgence in allowing me to remember an icon/iconoclast in real human terms. Now, I offer up a brief Smith bio-time line to help readers put into perspective some of Smith's Artistic manifestations so well chronicled in Anno's bibliography. Fittingly, Clark Ashton Smith makes his physical appearance on this earthly plane on the Friday the 13th of January, 1893 in the idyllic environs of Long Valley, California, U.S.A. (not too distant from rustic Auburn town). Clark had a peaceful childhood despite being beleaguered at times by illness. It has often been recounted how he educated himself by reading thoroughly items like the Encyclopedia Britannica (which he did twice). But, he also performed the daunting tasks as teaching himself, in his tender youth, Latin to the proficiency to being able to enjoy the classic Latin poets. Smith was an actual self-made and educated man who never lost sight of his true self including ever being autodidactic as he eventually refuses a prestigious Guggenheim Fellowship. Smith would later confide to close friends that the true reason for his refusal was that he didn't "want to become part of 'The Establishment'."

By the time CAS reaches his 11th year of existence, he is writing "imitations" of fairy tales and *The Arabian Nights* (the Richard Francis Burton annotated translation which Smith kept on his bookshelf all of his life) and, by age 17, Clark sells his first poems and four short stories to such magazines as the respected *Overland Monthly* and the popular pulp *Black Cat*.

It was the famed Mythologist/teacher Edith J. Hamilton who connects teenaged Clark with the unofficial Poet Laureate of the West Coast George Sterling and Smith would forever afterwards maintain a close relationship with that Romantic/Cosmic poet of note. At 19, CAS sees his stunning collection *The Star-Treader and Other Poems* published which, among others, delights Ambrose Bierce (who unfortunately just misses meeting the young talent face to face). In a mere three years, Star-Treader sells more than 1,000 copies which basically made it a 'best seller" of its time!

Smith was a gifted artist too and, in his twenties, has his "grotesque" paintings and drawings exhibited in New York City and highly admired West Coast art galleries (but he enjoyed more merely giving away his artistic endeavors rather than selling them). During this time period, in just ten days, a 27-year-old Clark writes what many consider his greatest long poem *The Hashish-eater; or The Apocalypse of Evil* that is a poetically rendered visage of his paintings.

In Smith's early 30's he learns French and translates Baudelaire. Almost foreshadowing his to be step-son's future fame, CAS works as a "poetic journalist" and does editing work for the *Auburn Journal* (mainly, though, to help pay off the expenses of his produced mammoth *Ebony and Crystal* poetry book). Some have wondered why such a sensitive poetic soul chose to remain in such a "backwater" area such as Auburn despite his numerous viral complaints on such an existence (CAS' personal letters reek with such sentiments).

If one spends some time (day and night) within the environment of the surrounding Sierra and its foothills, then a possible (though probably not the only motivation) answer can be encountered. The area is blessed ("cursed" as some Native American beliefs express) with an intangible (though sometimes very tangible) spirit that permeates the region right down to the very stones and minerals that so inspired Smith to sculpt his creations "Grotesques et Fantastiques." To use an overworked adjective, but it so fits, the area is primevally magical in nature. It reveals to those open and sensitive enough the influences that could inspire the production of tales like the *Genius Loci* and still enchant the resident!

An account told by several who closely knew Smith is an excellent example of this primevally mystical but real life realm's infusing potent power. At approximately 34, CAS was on one of his rock specimens searching modes along myth shrouded Crater Lake in the Sierra and he experiences what can easily be described as a transcendental moment. Clark is so touched by it that he produces one of his finest and poetic pieces of literature *The City of the Singing Flame* (a work that has gone on to influence and inspire the likes of Ray Bradbury and

Harlan Ellison).

Some, such as Smith scholar Lin Carter (editor and Introduction author to my edition of Zothique, among others in that adult fantasy series), have wondered about "causes" to why Smith, at a fairly early age, seemingly abruptly stops writing his speculative fiction. One of the reasons is that by age 45 Clark had become "disgusted" with the "limits" of pulp fantasy and how the writers were treated. So, until he reaches around age 48, Clark Ashton Smith decides to do "more living than writing."

In 1958, at 65, Clark makes his first and only television appearance on Sacramento's KCRA (Sacramento is the capital of California and not far from the foothills that house Auburn). It also set the stage for another of my Smith, Zothique and me encounters 20 years later. In 1978, KCRA sent a film crew et. al. to do a spot concerning Arkham Theatre. For the day of the filming, the AK gang decides to set up something nice and visual, so we chose my adaptation of Smith's Zothique tale (from my paperback) *Weaver In The Vault*. The ironic aspects come because after the shooting, the producer informs me about how the television station did a piece on Clark, then talks about how he was part of the production crew that taped it for a station's program and his pleasant memories of the man!

On August 14, 1961, aged 68, Clark Ashton Smith's physical being ceases its sojourn on this material plane and the Emperor of Dreams dies in his sleep. Still, Smith's Spirit continues its spells and within Anno Klarkash-Ton one will discover many a diverse hand and talent that has been so touched with the Smithian gift. Some comments anent concerning the contents.

Anno Klarkash-Ton is separated into various

sections that include poetry, a story, articles, art and a bibliography. As it suits Clark Ashton Smith's personal preference, the bulk of the material is poetry and such a wealth of scintillating versifiers are here. There are the exquisite poems from Leigh Blackmore, a gifted man who knows well the ways of the blood sorceress, the Goddess Spirit and the source of all things *Ubbo Sathla*. Pete Rawlik, David Schembri and Wade German treat us to glimpses of worlds and places that Smith would find succor as will we all in their respective *Hyperborean Lament*, *The Lord That Reigns Alone* and *Night Vigil for the Necromancer* (among others). Anno's own resident Enchantress Christene Britton-Jones returns us to CAS' darkly Romantic Averoigne territory (appropriate as Clark's family descended from Norman-French counts including the Hugunot Gaillards or Gaylords who came to new England in 1630) with her spell casting homage *The Lore of Averoigne*.

Judging from the output of stories and listed ideas created within Smith's various literary cycles, Zothique was his personal most visited locale. Ran Cartwright undoubtedly is one of the most knowledgeable tour guides today of that last continent providing us with such texts as his beloved *Tales of Zothique* and *Sorceries Gnydron* series (few may realize it, but Gnydron was Smith's original idea name for the land that became known as Zothique). Within Anno, Ran reintroduces us to his poetry talents as this time he escorts us to a moment in Hyperborea with his *Ilaiyana.*

Venerable poet Michael Fantina offers up several tribute poetry gems herein to Clark Ashton Smith such as his *C.A. Smith Emperor of Dreams*. Charles Baudelaire is credited with perfecting the often misunderstood and difficult to truly master form called the prose poem. Baudelaire had such influence on young Clark that he taught himself French, translated the majority of *Flowers of Evil* and mastered the prose poem for his own work. Two of the rare masters of the prose poem in their own right appearing in Anno Perry Grayson and W.H. Pugmire penned respectively *Emptiness* and *To Kiss Medusa* in honor of their muse Klarkash-Ton.

Charles Lovecraft has done much to keep Clark Ashton Smith's spirit alive including being the fine publisher of Anno Klarkash-Ton and Charle's poetry contributions to it display admirably why his book publications overall have such an artistic touch to them with his *A Wreath of Smithics for You, A Poppy Crown* (interesting note: Smith's lifelong home of California has as its state flower the Golden Poppy). *O Brother Spirit, Klarkash-Ton or The Hieroglypher Out of Time* (found within) by Henry Paget-Lowe is but another "nom de plume" for Charles Lovecraft. Also, thanks to Charles, Anno has the pleasure of housing Richard L. Tierney's *The Cave Wizard*.

As the founder/physical art creator of the *International Clark Ashton Smith Poetry Award* , I sincerely believe that, if it still existed today, the poetry found within this volume of Anno Klarkash-Ton would qualify to be nominated for that award. However, like CAS, who wrote stories and critiques as well, this volume contains some quality material of fiction and non-fiction.

Steve Lines is probably best known for his stunning artwork and indeed his covers (not to disregard Lines' very own signature stylings), for example, for Ran Cartwright's *Sorceries Gnydron* (and especially the Zothique series) are one of the closest today that really reflect the Smithian style. Besides Steve's art adorning Anno, the reader is also treated to his tale *The Eyes of the Scorpion*.

Frank Belknap Long, a published poet in his own right, actually knew Clark and provides a contemporary's critique with *The Poetry of Clark Ashton Smith* (another thank you here to Charles Lovecraft for making it available). I served on a Clark Ashton Smith panel at a World Fantasy Convention with Frank and to this day I remember what he said to me afterwards about his friend Klarkash-Ton, "He had the ability to make words transcend their symbols."

Redactor of Mhu Thulan Robert M. Price is no stranger to Klarkash-Ton with among his many achievements being the editor and introduction writer to the Chaosium Smith books including, of course, *The Klarkash-Ton Cycle* and *The Book of Eibon*. Price graces the pages of Anno with some more of his erudite insights with *Abhoth The Unclean*.

The multi-talented Brian M. Sammons provides the reader with one of his choice distinct reviews on one of the rare television adaptations of a Smith tale (perhaps, even giving an excellent example on why TV is oft called the "Boob Tube") with *A Seventies Sorcerer on the Small Screen*. It seems *The Return of the Sorcerer* met a better fate when dramatized on the 1940's popular radio show *The House of Mystery*.

Anno has been blessed with being able to include some insightful articles, such as "Clark Ashton Smith in Carmel," by the highly regarded CAS scholar/authority Scott Connors, who was an editor of such publications as the *Selected Letters of Clark Ashton Smith*. There is almost an irony connected to the story about Clark's visit as Pacific Grove, the location of his wife Carol's home where he spend his last days, is situated right next door to Carmel.

After being enchanted by all of those CAS inspired manifestations, Anno provides one of the most precise sources for the reader to seek out the material that planted the seeds with its *Bibliography and Checklist.* It was compiled with the loving hands and scholarly minds of the incomparable Smith sages Glynn Owen Barrass and Edward P. Berglund. In my opinion Anno Klarkash-Ton is the best of its kind since the publication of *The Emperor of Dreams* edited by Donald Sydney-Fryer.

Typical of those of the Auburn area who remember Smith is Persia Woolley's singular image of "a solitary man who walked the Auburn Folsom Road from his cabin to town, wearing a beret and seemingly engrossed in far distant thoughts." Clark Ashton Smith/Klarkash-Ton no longer walks alone.

- Frederick J. Mayer –

POETRY

TO CLARK ASHTON SMITH
Leigh Blackmore

Oh, Emperor of poetry sublime!
Oh, Bard of Auburn, seer of many things!
Thy pen has told with wit that sears and stings
Of shapes that lie within Poe's "wild, weird clime."
Your vision compassed dying stars and suns
That reel and totter down the aisles of space;
And with acerbic eye you viewed our race—
Its petty dreams your poetry outruns.

With gilded pen you traced transcendent realms—
Vast worlds senescent, poisoned blossoms rife,
Exotic scenes of unfamiliar life.
Like ghostly ships with dead men at their helms
Your tales sail on, apocalyptic, old
Beyond the telling – veins of purest gold!

- 5L -

UBBO-SATHLA

Leigh Blackmore

In steaming fens and mires of primal Earth,
The efts of terrene life are spawned and spread;
A formless mass bulks large on the swamp-bed,
The loathsome Source whence all are given birth.
Some, aeons later, take the form of man,
Unconscious of to what they owe their mind –
An idiotic morass, star-born, blind –
And this, part only of the Great Ones' plan.

New England graves, the earth new-turned and fresh.
Lie in the rain as mourners walk away,
Unwilling to dwell too long on the way
The maggot now corrupts the stinking flesh.
Nor he who lives, nor rots, suspects – but learns –
To Ubbo-Sathla every life returns

LORE OF AVEROIGNE
Christene Britton-Jones

That ancient tales and lore tell of Averoigne
Is neither past nor present but here evermore
Not a past relic but alive in the moonlight of Ximes.
Dead or living Loup Garous and witchcraft abound
Which quoth Sier du Malinbous "was timely indeed."
Can Gaspard du Nord of Vyone's ancient reign swear
Eternal to the French cult of Sadoqua all powerful
Lie sentient till summoned by *The Book of Eibon.*

And Druids of Averoigne revered the god's utterances
With stone tablets of Atlantean high priest Klarkash-Ton
Strange dark deeds through the past millennium
Aeons preceded when Liber Ivonis speaks in 2012
Even *Chateau Des Faussesflames* crumbled and fell
Death came upon Abbey Perigon not from the sky.
May the worshipping of Sadoqua in medieval times
Die not in memory of yore for the Old Ones waken today.

ILAIYANA
Ran Cartwright

Ilaiyana.
Beautiful Ilaiyana.
The last of her kind; the last High Priestess of the Cult of Yhoundeh.
Now she is dead.
I know…
I, faithful servant of Tsathoggua, slit her throat with my knife.
But it was an act of kindness, not vengeance as some would say; yes, kindness it was.
She, High Priestess of Yhoundeh, captive of our priesthood, was sentence to
      die; if die she would; could.
In the Valley of Whispers.
Take her there to die! the Tsathogguan High Priest proclaimed.
Let It do to her what it shall.
It.
Not Tsathoggua.
No, it was something else, a thing unknown.
There were legends. Yes, there were stories.
A black shape, amorphous…
Some laughed. I didn't.
We took her to the Valley of Whispers, stripped her, strung her up by her wrists to a pole
      of wood…and left her alone as the night came.
Shadows clawed the blasted valley.

We stayed close; to hear, not to see, and we heard. Yes, we heard.

Ilaiyana's hideous screams.

Terror.

Torment.

Madness.

All through the night.

A thing that called her name whispered on the wind in the Valley of Whispers.

Ilaiyana, It called.

Ilaiyana.

It howled a distant mad cackling laughter,

Sent her voice to high pitched hoarse shrieks the likes of which no man or beast had ever

     made.

Then the sun rose on the morn.

Still she shrieked and cackled and shrieked and cackled with terror filled madness.

We crept in close, cautious; fearful.

If that thing were to be lurking… But it was gone.

She hung by her wrists still; hair now wild, unkempt, snow white; skin snow white; black

     circles around her eyes.

Her beauty vanished in a night.

Still she shrieked; and cackled.

Babbled madness.

Horrible madness.

Hideous madness.

It was in her eyes, her wild eyes, what she had seen in the night.

It.

A thing unknown, but now known to her.

I could stand no more; I pulled my knife, rushed to her

side, and raked the blade across
        her throat.
Sprayed crimson; washed down the whiteness of her
neck, her naked breasts.
A sudden wild distant howl I heard that no one else
heard.
A distant thunderous echo in the air that no one else
heard.
My name whispered on the wind in the Valley of
Whispers that no one else heard.
I dropped my knife and fled.
Alone.
Across the blasted valley.
Now the night falls soon; I hear It whisper my name.
It comes. Soon.
A thing unknown.
The shadows, they move, closer.
Closer...

EMPTINESS
A POEM IN PROSE
By Perry M. Grayson

The traveller recited the words to inner ears. His heels pounded the pavement hard, and in his mind the Rebel's written edict blares. 'The gods are dead, the earth has covered them,' was scrawled to print three quarter centuries gone. Pale deities lay deceased much longer still. "Far less they are," the traveller sighed, "than shadows in man's narrow sight. This land is empty to me now; it stands bereft of wonderment." The Traveller cursed such urban blight, the advertisements so impish, trite. "The sky is blank and patternless; it looks down on egocentric homes. Self-centred greed for designer lives, holier than thou games in their bitter hive. Never considering an ounce of compassion around, their fate to mire in vicious quag." The hills and fields all blocked from view, beyond iron gates, no green hue. A haughty trend-follower demeans and berates the Traveller in abject dismay. He doesn't belong here, he's left behind— this straggler of forgotten time. The Traveller knows he must endure, although devoid of aged lore. And turning his back upon wretched abodes, he spies three cockroaches creeping low. They hiss atop a power box, subsisting on dimming city lots. The traveller ignores their faecal trail, and beats his wings towards willowed dales.

12

NIGHT VIGIL FOR THE NECROMANCER

Wade German

I have here, master, leaves from your grimoire;
And by their elder glyphs and diagrams,
The arcane, overlapping pentagrams,
Surmise you voyage now the farthest shores
Where, singing spells of great antiquity,
You search for stranger necromantic lore
And chart the death dimension and its doors,
Those barriers between realities.

In your high castle carved from crystal verse,
A spectral servant waits for your return,
And speculates on what his lord might learn
In far, occult infinities immersed,
Where alien worlds emerge from nighted streams,
The unknown gulfs in nebulae of dream.

14

TO KISS MEDUSA
BY W. H. Pugmire

Mauve sky, and seven incandescent spheres that hang in heaven, cosmic baubles with which the gods may play. From some distant place, a hymn is played to Pan, delicately fluted and yet containing an undertone of mischievous menace. I do not now recall how I came to this place. It may have been that I walked through banks of cloud, airy portals; or perhaps I have split a seam of dreaming and stepped between dimensions with limbs less than mortal. I stepped beyond mauve sky, to an under-ground hallway of delirium, chthonic nightmare clutching at my length of hair. You are there, at the end of the passageway, magnificent and immortal upon your dais. How strange to see that you, the fantastic symbol, have been rendered into an eikon of stone, that substance into which they who feasted on your magnificent horror were altered. I see their remnants littered all around you, the shattered and the broken figures of soldiers, princes, knaves. They lie as stones adorned with your leprous touch of Death, and their determined valour is replaced with grimaces of horror.

You stand upon your dais, your head slightly askew. And I see the crack that separates your neck from the rest of you, that place of wound where one clever fellow killed you. I walk to you in that hallway that is your grotto, and I am nude except for the garland of dead serpents, those lean dry corpses that weave into my length of hair. I press my breasts to yours and touch your mouth with mine.   Whispering, I name thee.   My acolyte's kiss is liquid, living. My witch hands smooth the crack beneath your neck with healing. Your serpents twine with mine as we exchange places. I stand upon the dais and peer into your awful beauty, and I am glad to feel my liquid lips grow dry as my flesh, that mortal sheath, gradually transforms and turns to stone.

HYPERBOREAN LAMENT
By Pete Rawlik

On Voormadrith as in Mhu Thulan,
The ebon glaciers doth creep,
Through crevices of stone and forests,
Monstrously slow do they seep.

The wasted streets of Uzuldaroum,
Do howl with lonely winds,
Round fools who stood to fight the cold,
And stand frozen for their sins.

While in the sea, Yikilth, the floating ice,
Doth flounder, fester and reek,
While the pale slug, Rlim Shaikorth,
Coils round that frozen peak.

Men driven from the frosted lands,
The Voormis rise in a macabre hurrah,
Their young consigned to frigid flame,
The conquering ice Aphoom Zhah!

AMONGST THE STARS I DREAM
By Pete Rawlik

On the edge of the horizon,
just a hint of light so faint there.
With the dawn the world is pregnant, oh
have I been gone so long?

Once again my night has been stolen
by the dark and twinkling sky,
I've been dreaming without sleeping,
I have walked in Morpheus' fold.

I have soar'd an unknown skyline,
on a pair of equine wings there.
I have quenched my aching throat
from the water bearer's jug.
And I wrestled Ursa Minor
to be chased off by her mate,
and my horoscope I read there
glancing o'er Orion's shoulder.
And once, just once I danced there
'gainst the breast of Andromeda,
oh so softly kissed her starry lips,
just once there in the darkness.

But I don't think I shall dream anymore,
not for a while now,

I had forgotten Andromeda,
Perseus' lady represents,
and buried deep
in Perseus' sack
He guards the Gorgon's head.

On the edge of the horizon,
just a hint of light so faint there.
With the moon the world is pregnant, oh
have I been gone so long?

Once again my day has been stolen
by the shuffling of papers,
in the sky the stars are calling
but I really should not go

Now I am flying up on swan's wings
darting just between the Twins there,
and I watch as Lion chases
Aires round the Virgin Child.
Then softly, very softly
the Seven Sisters whisper
and direct my nightly journey
to behind the Balanced Scales
And I listen to the Lute
as once more I find myself
twixt Andromeda's arms

But I don't think I shall dream anymore,
not for a while now,
I had forgotten Andromeda,
Perseus' lady represents,
and buried deep

in Perseus' sack
He guards the Gorgon's head.

On the edge of the horizon,
just a hint of light so faint there.
With the sky the world is pregnant, oh
have I been gone so long?

All my nights they are stolen,
by jealous vengeful stars.
I sleep without dreaming
My eyes are forever drawn.

Starry wings are just a fantasy
and the Cross is just a shape now.
Hercules just a star
and Mars a cold, cold stone

And I stand here in silence,
in my garden I stand watch,
as the stars they shift alignments
and I whisper, nearly silent
to milady Andromeda.

But I don't think I shall dream anymore,
not for a while now,
I had forgotten Andromeda,
Perseus' lady represents,
and buried,
not so deep
in Perseus' sack
He guards the Gorgon's head.

THE LORD THAT REIGNS ALONE
By David Schembri

'Tis my home beneath a veil of dust,
Desolate and snowless,
Volcanic craters like hungry mouths,
I live alone and forgotten – powerless.

The vast lakes I once knew
Now fathomless gulfs – barren and dry,
Depths of sullen blackness and ashen air,
I am bereft of moisture to cry.

For aeons I have stared upon my crumbled
      throne,
Remains of my sweet queen, dearest and
      dead,
The bones of my kindred, the men that
were,
Lay rotten in my land from feet to head.

I wander amongst the swirling sand,
My eyes dim and blind,
Yet a dense shadow desolate to the sun,
Cast by a gigantean of stone – I gasp to
find.

The towering mass of enormous heights,

Its peak shrouded by angry clouds,
My mind feels the subtle hope – salvation?
Since been lost beneath an eternal shroud.

I mount the rough and cracked stone,
Climbing for the summit, battling biting
cold,
Endless hours through dregs of darkness
and   blinding light,
I hunger for the freedom through the gates
of   old.

Through my difficult accent, I am left weak
        and stranded,
With the sullen black world beneath,
I stare vertically for hours, fingers buried in
t   he cracks,
My slightest of hope is but grey with grief.

I am dry and brittle, leather on bones,
My every joint brings an agonizing sting,
I need life force – mortal blood,
Only that warm thick nectar could revive
this   king!

I summon to the heights, the mortal
kingdom,
From a fallen Lord who reigns alone,
My final breath, its seductive haze,
I need but one touch upon this stone.

But, Ah, the lovely allure forces a mortal
        hand,

Their light caress to turn their face pale,
Their blood falls the deep descent,
I press closer in eagerness so the river shalt
        not fail.

Through my dry veins travels the warm
        savage juice,
My accent is quick and cunning,

I roar to the great heights above,
"Beware for I am a-coming!"

'Twas my home that bore lanterns of light,
'Til the skin-clad savages came and began
        their fight,
Raging their war, their swords blood
        drenched,
Turning us voiceless, lifeless, and death-
        clenched.

My sudden eruption into their skies,
        Soaring, a-crying
With thunderbolts through my hands,
        I shall be the dark deliverer
Never night nor day disturb,
        Laying my brutal vengeance upon
these lands.

THE TORTURER'S OATH
By David Schembri

Come with me, dear Sir, simply follow my voice,
The blindfold leaves you shrouded in mystery,
Bereft of sight and choice,
Enter my chamber, my secret place; a domain of eternal
      sin,
Allow me to uncover your eyes, sit you down,
Now, we must begin.

Forgive the dimness to this room,
I will light a candle and present my tools,
Look here!
See numerous implements fit for surgeons,
And where you sit – 'tis my loyal stool.

Let me fasten your shins and wrists,
Notch by notch – strong and tight,
Draw your fearful eyes to my dear friend at your feet,
My hungry and rusted vice!

Questions shall come later, so silence your tongue, 'tis
my   advice,
You dealt in business that made me look the fool,
So for that, dear Sir,
You must first pay the price.

See my rusted, crimson friend,
Its metal lips hungry and wide,

24

Let me secure your right foot behind its teeth,
Press in the bolted clamps at its side.

I turn the lever, slow and sure,
Allowing your shin to turn as red as a rose,
Yes, I hear your screams – the tearing; the crunch!
I shall not stop until the metal lips are closed.

There now, draw your breath,
Your dues are surely paid,
You must see the result of your suffering,
I insist!
Let us look down at what we have made.

Allow me to assist you forward,
Guide your head down against your will,
Let me loosen the brace, shift your leg,
For beyond the cold lips –
'tis your foot, limp and still.

We are far from anywhere,
You and I,
Through twisted wood and hidden trail,
You can scream all you wish,
It will be but an echo
through this secret dale.

I found your letters to my wife,
Episodes of passion and clandestine cheers,
I have read every one of them; I would have you know,
They dated back for years.

But, you see, Leonard,

I care not for this pitiful affair –
Ethel has packed and left!
There is a sudden absence to my wealth;
I know I am the victim
of a filthy theft!

So, disclose to me now,
Where is dear Ethel?
Give her up, you gallant fool!
Or I shall unleash every craft in my chamber,
And dissect you in my stool!

Ah, the valley, you say? With a river nearby?
'Twas the manor where we were wed,
Little does she know,
What I do now, I did back then –
I forged that house long before
our union was said.

For in the south wing – beneath the stairs,
Lives a deep passage
through a catacomb or two,
There dwells a chamber just like this,
Where I shall question Ethel,
Just as I have done you.

THE CAVE WIZARD
(DEDICATED TO CLARK ASHTON SMITH)
By Richard L. Tierney

Within old Auburn's aureate hills
    The mad encaverned wizard dwells.
Beneath the moon he chants and shrills,
    Brewing philtres, casting spells.

Within his dank and umbrous cave
    He crafts his blasphemous statuettes
While townsfolk cringe to hear him rave
    From out his echoing oubliettes.

They know full well each chanted howl
    Is conjuring up an evil shade
Whose shambling lich will rise to prowl
    Beneath the moon's ensanguined blade.

INSPIRED BY CLARK ASHTON SMITH

Michael Fantina

THE MUSE*

Far from environs of our boiling sun,
She fled from me to realms ineffable
To silken seas those restless tides foretell,
Awakening some new Leviathan,
Where lurching mountains mauve and cinnamon
Throw shadows on the moorland and the fell,
Where grow the amaranth and asphodel,
It's here she leaves me to oblivion.

And yet within my deepest black despair,
When all is lost and I am faced with doom,
I know her scent, thick in the midnight air,
Her rare and most enchanting strong perfume,
Then I grow giddy, all my head's aswirl,
She has come back, my Muse, my fickle girl!

*Inspired by CAS's sonnet "Absence of the Muse"

C.A. SMITH EMPEROR OF DREAMS

On ebon headlands thrusting to the gloom
Of ancient seas grown self aware and dire,
Burns bright the flame from his tall slender pyre,
With frankincense and myrrh and rare perfume.
Below the steep cliff's gulfs the boom, boom, boom
Of combers come to see that dancing spire,
And churn below that most stupendous fire,
Like mourners to some frequented high tomb.

His travels long ago have left this world
To soar among the oldest triple stars,
In spans of Space secluded and apart
Where star streams pale as milk will furl, unfurl,
Their distant glow like to wan silver bars,
Which somehow soothe and gladden all the heart.

A TRIBUTE TO
CLARK ASHTON SMITH
(1893—1961)

I waited till the fallen clamours died,
One scarlet eve when they lay drunk with wine,
The sated king, his whore and concubine,
There on the palace floor where grey ghosts glide.
From out my mouldered tomb this night I ride,
His murdered love, for vengeance on this swine,
My liege, so treacherous, morose, malign,
I come this night like an avenging tide!

That dawn they found my liege a pile of dust,
And swiftly blown across the palace floors,
No trace but memory and his lost lust
There scattered through the polished corridors,
Though on November nights may yet be seen,
My tall and regal ghost, his former queen.

FOR CLARK ASHTON SMITH (1893—1961)

My concubines all made of frailest air,
Like pretty smoke they drift above these streams,
When winter rules, or in the sultry steams
Of summer's heat and comb their gorgeous hair.
I am alone, and to my cave repair
When storms arise to blow away these themes,
I watch in silence all my avid dreams
File past me in a whirlwind of despair.

A monarch whose great name is long forgot
And only dead men lisp it silently,
What's left of me is merely mould and rot,
My city foundered in the deepest sea,
And yet at night I see mine ancient realm
Glide like some ship, and I am at the helm.

FLAME*

Thy love is like a spell well cast
Of which the darkling mages tell,
So erudite, ineffable,
And conjured from the icy vast.

About your throat that precious jewel
Wherein the spells of Paradise
Reflect the colour of your eyes,
Each precious pretty drowning pool.

You've called me by my secret name,
Beyond all vasts, beyond all ploys,
Your love ennui it bends, destroys,
With your most holy, hidden flame.

*inspired by Smith "Ineffability".

A WREATHE OF SMITHICS FOR YOU, A POPPY CROWN

Charles Lovecraft

THE WIZARD OF THE AUBURN HILLS

Within the Auburn hills a wizard waits
   Wrapped up in spells and philtres dark and dead;
   Always from his old voice of morbid dread
The runes of sound arise which sane men hate.
Near half a century ago the fate
   Of this leagued warlock dark, by dark dreams fed,
   Arose to hie him glimpses coveted
In fields of amaranth where meet the late.

Onwards the powers of the dark augment
   Forever in our perilous world, bait
      Of those mad callers of the black thereof,
To take, and chew and gouge their souls; relent
   Only the few who magic's power prove.
      Thus in the Auburn hills a wizard waits.

EVERYTHING IS BROKEN

The broken spheres, the gyres of time, the mists
And haze of worlds dissolved in fading golds,
The long lost emperies diseased and cold
Whose gelid kalpas reignless there persist;
Eyries of battlements by dead moons kissed
And lost, mid faltering beams of cracked gems old,
And dusted with dire gases of night's fold,
The ageless hours of infinitude list.

The cogs that worked once wholly wrecked now are.
Inimical in time's great gallery
The torn off masks of gaunt stars leer down screes,
Whilst catafalques of time like dozers star.
What hectic wreckages have now wrought there
The broken-off ends of the starry stair.

CAS

Tours through the void; the soft parade a-rush
In its far, intricate night swirls. A thing,
A-spill with radiant gold dusts glimmering,
Brings some strange usher of the night time hush.
The velvet dark encroaches with a gush,
As if a stone were struck, dream following.
With masterful intent these vales you bring,
Then lord thou over them as one dream pushed.

As some epochal guide the lanterns start
At your approach. They flare right near your feet
As you pass brushing odd things where dreams meet,
Near crossroads of all kinds which sight impart.
With coruscating eyes the lamps, the tours,
The opalescent fires that burn, are yours.

THE BIBLIOTAPH

This lineage out of time, the molecules
Dissolve in vats of fluid dark. How start
The chaos-bending joys which fear imparts
To those dull wriggling lines, the tiny ampoules
Red, in their old, prosaic, archaic Yules.
In my strong hands their sources break apart,
And sorcerers bow down bereft of hearts,
And bugs are tortured on lost graticules.

Here my observance calms. In this cool place
The floor to ceiling and the wall to wall
Wide stacks of rotting books my sense withal
Assail, with smells' corruptive pail of space;
Whilst there upheld, writ large, the glyphs of time
Shine on in starry sorceries sublime.

O BROTHER SPIRIT,
KLARKASH-TON;
OR, THE HIEROGLYPHER OUT OF TIME
(Henry Paget-Lowe)

You transport far our withered brains as if
In canisters were strung our minds through space.
The coruscations of that elder lace
Are eyes which tell all things, as in *Azif*.
But you have made of them a timeless zenith
Of the archaic zones, an archway traced
With figured poetry and starlight faced
Embroidery stitched straight on Night's black pith.

What dawns unparalleled unveiled down halls
Empowered dark. Unheralded the lamps
Of thy deep violescent eyes like falls
Rushed down toad-like eternities encamped.
Ah, brother spirit Klarkash Ton, none strike
Those notes so well; of *ye* there's few the like!

LOVECRAFT WAS RIGHT

How rich the setting suns of your lost worlds.
　　With eyes that float in pools of lotus dreams
　　With petals of the large bright floating schemes
You carry us where harlequins have swirled
Their mantles of prismatic views unfurled,
　　And lay for us the wreathes of crystal beams
　　All cracked with icy gem-fire inlaid streams
For our strange passing where we head, space hurled.

But few have spied those deadly vistas rear.
Their sheens of poisonous exotic blooms
That you have known with maddening perfumes
Your brother and you only have seen there.
　　Lovecraft was right. What visions ineluctable
　　Are yours, what alien vistas quite incomparable!

THE LOST WORLD OF SMITH

How swirl the setting suns of your lost worlds.
   They spin in all their soft chromatic sprees,
   Dramatic colorations that make see
      The eyes which through them peer from cool host
wolds.

How deep the tempera of your lost worlds,
   O emperor of dreams, to lay on us
   Their setting tints forever in a fuss
      Of odorous vapours' clinging rising holds.

How rich the strange pavane of your lost worlds
   That circle like the ever circling skulls
   Of lotus realms which have died there, the hulls
      Of vivid voids incomparable in mold.

How sunset rimmed and steeped are your lost worlds,
   Vicissitudes of daring explorations,
   The voids fill with your cryptic resonations;
      Like tapers shine the vacuum's burning cold.

How seething are the teeth of your lost worlds
   To gnash the voids and dreamers who stream through
   To be all starlit there, one of the few
      Who came back sane to be the one who told.

Forever are the suns of your lost worlds
   To come and go far overhead in voids

Of pendulums that hover planetoids
  On which pale life and light grow deadly bold.

FOR SMITH

Thy crystal sonnets, O Clark Ashton Smith,
    Thine ebony and crystal sonnets breathe.
The tinctured rim of your great work is kith
    To the harmonious joyance we receive
    In Shelley's and in Keats's work. We grieve
There was not even more, O wild word-smith,
    To catch us and to carry us where wreathes
Olympian the foreheads crown forthwith,
    And even as up there they wildly weave.
Your quill, the well of your strange fingertips,
    The will you wield to daub clouds on blue sheathes
With wild prismatic paint, the ink you dip.
    The structured train of your great works reminds
    Us yet again to value all your kind.

FICTION

THE EYES OF THE SCORPION
Steve Lines

Harken unto me O true believers, for I, Khalik, shall relate the marvelous adventure of the Eyes of the Scorpion. Know you that I was living a most contented and luxurious existence in Sharador, spreading largesse and rejoicing over my sizeable gains and profits... and these made largely at the expense of the Caliph of Shondar Zal. I abode a while in the municipality savouring the utmost ease and prosperity until I was once more seized with a yearning for travel and did crave after adventure and lucre and emolument.

Learning that the Sultan Ali Hassan was travelling with his royal caravan into the desolate northern lands to trade concubines and marmalukes with the Sultan of Sharaz, one Zoolim Roob, I did resolve also to embark upon this venture and thus I presented myself to Ali Hassan, kissing the ground between my hands, and offering my services as royal bodyguard. The Sultan knew me to be a sworder of great renown, for in times past I had quested in his service and braved perils beyond measuring, and in an instant he did appoint me personal guardian to his court magician, the necromancer Zarallu.

Few, if any, had beheld Zarallu, for he spent his time ensconced in the topmost room of the highest tower of the palace of Ali Hassan. I had but glimpsed him once, abroad in the ravaged night, while fretted clouds scudded across a thrashing, stormy sky. I was engaged in the quest for the stolen soul of Jamilla, when I beheld the necromancer, cloaked and shrouded in shadow, striding though the rotting cemeteries of Zarathis. I noted that at his passing the graves and sepulchres trembled and shook and I discerned vague movement amid the tombs. I saw no more, for I was about my quest, but it seemed to me that the restless dead did seek to rise beneath the leering moon and follow in Zarallu's wake.

However, I had encountered the living dead before, not least when upon my quest for the Sacred Parchment of Jalur, upon the isle of Vhakhla. And so, the guarding of the necromancer, while unpalatable, afforded me no measurable distress. Though why he should wish to venture from his seclusion was a mystery beyond supposition.

Thus it was that I spent a small time purchasing the necessaries for a long voyage and then rode my Perushian stallion through the winding streets and alleys to join the Sultan's caravan as it departed the great city of Sharador through the north gate.

1. The Haunted Necropolis

Far we travelled across the lands of Perushia, for Ali Hassan drove his caravan hard. I rode upon my faithful steed, cantering behind the purple draped carriage of the mysterious Zarallu. He would regard me inscrutably on occasion from between the folds of cloth, his unseen face ever in shadow, but not one word had the mage uttered since I had joined the caravan.

Oftimes as we rode I would gaze ahead at the silk

enwrapped carriages which held the Sultan's most beauteous concubines, occasionally catching a quick glimpse of khol-lined eyes peeking at me with amusement, as dainty, pale hands parted the silks. Fancies filled my mind...daydreams of warm scented evenings spent rolling amid the silken pillows of my own seraglio, my every whim ministered to by these Houris in human guise. In truth however, even to gaze upon the unveiled faces of the Sultan's concubines meant instant death, and the guards about the carriage; the Sultan's own Red Guard, were ever vigilant. I knew that such as they had no interest in female pulchritude.

In the cool evenings we would unfurl the tents and pavilions and I would unroll my carpets and take my brief rest, placing my mats across the entrance to Zarallu's black pavilion, a dwelling second only in stature to the purple and yellow pavilion of Ali Hassan. As the camp fell slowly to slumber I, in contrast, would awaken and take my position as guard outside the ebon tent, my thoughts only occasionally straying to that fleeting sight of Zarallu amongst the tombs of Zarathis.

*   *   *

And so we travelled. As day followed day we crossed the jewelled lands of fair Perushia and passed eventually into bordering Samarzul. After a time we drew nigh the borders of Khofar and came then upon the great desert wastes of Zambi.

In the market places of Kazrah tales were spun of ancient legends which told that deep within this arid desert, beyond the fathomless ravines of Ulthaz, there was said to lie Khanazur, an ancient and dis-remembered necropolis, lost these thousand years amid the ever shifting sands. Those creatures that dwelt still within its crumbling, fretted walls were ghuls so it was related; devourers of carrion, and it was known to be a city of the dead and accursed by Zallah.

*   *   *

Now it happened that, after much adventure and no small measure of conflict with the winged Harzool, those crimson demons that infested the twisting ravines of Ulthaz, the caravan of the Sultan chanced upon a great city thrusting its crumbling towers from the rolling dunes. A hushed silence fell upon all and praises were offered to Zallah, for this could be no other place than the legend-haunted necropolis of Khanazur, Lost City of the Dead!

Dusk was approaching as we beheld this morbid sight and the dying sun cast its sanguine glow upon the decaying walls that rose from the ashen sand and it seemed to my dark eyes that the dead city did lay bathed in blood!

Nonetheless, despite this most inauspicious omen, Ali Hassan ordered camp to be made without the silent city's mouldering walls and so it was that tents were erected and campfires soon burning.

As the curtains of twilight fell, strange stories were told around the fires and frightened, superstitious eyes would oft glance furtively at the shadowed walls of Khanazur and many prayers were offered to Zallah for succour and salvation.

Once again, after my customary brief slumber, I took my place without the black pavilion of Zarallu.

50

2. The Tale of Jamal

As I stood guard, my eyes straying toward that ominous city of death, I heard the ribald laughter of a group of merchants who sat gathered about a nearby fire. Their spirits were quickened by wine and hashish and their voices grew in volume so that I clearly discerned their heated converse.

"Cur of a dog!" spake one. "Why dost thou mock me Sanjar? It is as I have related, by Zallah. Heed my words, for verily it is true, although only Zallah is all-knowing."

"Say you so, Jamal?" sneered the other. "All know the Eyes of the Scorpion are but legend; an opium dream spun by dull eyed mendicants to fleece ignorant peasants."

"Not so, Sanjar," spake Jamal. "For the tale of The Eyes of the Scorpion was handed down to me by my father and to him by his father and so back into the past of dim remembering."

"Say on then, Jamal. Spill your fancy tale for all to hear."

Jamal began his story: "It is said that in days of yore and ages long gone, evil Khanazur was a flourishing metropolis; the confluence of many trade routes, and countless were the caravans who visited her, for she was builded beside a mighty oasis. Its citizens, however, were jealous and ruthless in the way of business and were in the habit of taking advantage of honest merchants who chanced in their direction. Now there came a time when a caravan most strange approached the limits of Khanazur. It came from an area of the desert where few merchants had ever ventured and none had ever returned, for it was

51

said to be accursed by Zallah.

"A train of black camels padded through the streets and all the populace stood in silent awe and watched as this grim, ebon hued caravan entered the city. There was about it an air of death and decomposition. As well as being of unusual hue the camels were skeletal of frame and their eyes smouldered with a scarlet fire. The caravans were decorated with the accoutrements of the tomb and pallid cerements flapped in the arid desert breeze. Those who rode the black beasts or walked by their sides were likewise robed in shrouds of funerary hue, their faces concealed, (though whether this was against the glare of the desert sun, the bite of wind blown sand, or the gaze of the curious onlookers none could say). Their gait was most strange, for their movements were uncertain and haphazard, as though the act of perambulation was new to them.

"By all these things, (and the noxious stench of corruption), it was known by all that this was the caravan of a necromancer."

"Zallah curse you Jamal," growled the one known as Sanjar. "We seek not a lesson in history! What of the Eyes of the Scorpion?"

"Still thy flapping tongue Sanjar or by Zallah my blade will anoint thy swarthy neck with a crimson kiss!"

At this, Sanjar fell silent, dark eyes glaring, while Jamal continued his tale: "It transpired as I have related. The necromancer Shalla Bey had come to Khanazur. I shall shorten my discourse for the benefit of those ignorant curs amongst you who like not a majestic tale, savoured in the telling." At this Jamal gestured at Sanjar. "Let it be known that Shalla Bey did walk amongst the people of Khanazur and all knew fear at his

52

manifestation. He stood two heads taller than the tallest man in Khanazur, though his frame was emaciated unto the appearance of a desert lich. His hair hung long and lank from his cranium and cascaded about his shoulders and it was as white as a virgin's dreams. His crimson eyes burned with an unholy flame and were such that none could hold his gaze for more than a moment. He wore cerements and shrouds, soiled and torn, as though newly ravished from ancient tombs. This was Shalla Bey!

"The necromancer ordered the raising of a mighty temple in the center of Khanazur, builded by the labor of liches, called from the cemeteries of the desert by Shalla Bey's necromantic powers. And this temple was for the adoration of the vile god of the desert sands, the Scorpion God Girtab. Awesome and terrible was this mighty fane, black as the desert night with a mighty dome held aloft by six slender pillars and within that monumental fane, deep underground, it is said that Shalla Bey caused an eidolon to be constructed, fashioned from adamant black as the heart of Shaizan. This statue was in the manner of a dark scorpion, vicious tail raised high, and it stood thrice the height of a man and was twenty paces in length. By means of evil sorceries had this eidolon been constructed and at its feet thousands would be slain in adoration of Girtab, The Scorpion God, for Shalla Bey decreed he was the one true god.

"And so it was that Khanazur festered under the yoke of the malign necromancer Shalla Bey.

"Every month at the blooming of the moon, sacrifices were made upon the altar of the Scorpion God. Acrid fumes would rise from the temple and tortured screams of agony and despair would taint the desert night and with each sacrificial death given in the honour of

Girtab so would there be one more lich at the command of the necromancer.

"Caravans avoided the accursed city and in time the desert sands drank the cool waters and scoured the lush vegetation from the land, and the once great oasis slowly dwindled. Thus it was that once mighty Khanazur fell into ruin and despair. Sustenance grew scarce and Shalla Bey did naught to assuage the hunger of his people for his undead slaves did not require food and the necromancer sustained his unnatural vitality with strange drugs and potions. It was whispered that he had walked the avenues of legend haunted Voorzoth, which fell into ruin over a thousand years ago.

"After a time, all wholesome provender was exhausted within the city and the starving populace of Khanazur, tainted by the corruption of the necromancer, began to surreptitiously abduct the undead servitors of Shalla Bey and feast upon their stringy flesh. And so it was that, with the unfolding of time, the denizens of Khanazur became foul ghuls who thirsted for the meat of mankind and thus became accursed in the eyes of Zallah who caused them to copulate with the hyenas and jackals of the desert until their offspring took on the aspect of dogs and the populace of the doomed metropolis forever abandoned the ways of decent men.

"Shalla Bey cared not, for ghuls were as able servitors as liches and by their hunger for flesh more readily governed. Thus it was that Khanazur became a city of the dead whose sovereign was a necromancer and whose populace was ghuls and the unquiet dead."

"Zallah curse you, Jamal! What of the Eyes of the Scorpion?" Sanjar rose to his feet shouting: "What of The Eyes of the Scorpion?"

Jamal fingered his scimitar suggestively and Sanjar returned to his carpet. "Patience my eager friend. It is related," Jamal continued, "that with the unfolding of the years the mangy ghuls in the employ of Shalla Bey did consume all living flesh 'til naught remained within the confines of the city save the ghuls and the undead. This caused unrest amongst the carrion curs, for the meat of the perambulating liches was tough and stringy and the contents of the several cemeteries without the city had been long consumed. Shalla Bey, aware of this discontent realized that things could not continue thus for much longer and did engage in powerful sorceries and magicks strange and rare and did cause the occasional caravan to come to Khanazur, thus providing the restless ghuls with fresh meat and flowing blood. However, this was not enough to assuage the incessant hunger of the ghuls who had fairly decimated the ranks of the undead in Shalla Bey's employ.

Jamal paused and looked suggestively at Sanjar. "And now I come to the point of my tale. The Temple of the Scorpion lay deep in the heart of the city, as I have related, and it is said that there came a day when Shalla Bey realized that the span of his mortal life was drawing to a close, despite his vile sorceries, and he did visit the fane of the Scorpion God and knelt before the representation of his god in humble prayer. After paying homage to Girtab, Shalla Bey did then eloign to his private chambers where he remained ensconced for the duration of forty days and forty nights. During this while strange creatures loped in from the desert 'neath the uncertain starlight and entered the necromancer's chambers. Miasmic emanations clouded and tainted the air and horrific shrieks and screams were heard continuously, day and night…some say they were the rantings of Shalla Bey himself, others that he conjoined with Jinn and Peris in unholy copulations.

"Whatever: after the duration related, the necromancer exited his chambers, presenting an aspect most horrific, for his frame, already gaunt was now as emaciated and pale as those of his undead servitors. His crimson eyes burned feverishly and his gaunt face wore an expression of evil triumph. Curious ghuls followed as he again entered the Black Temple and, standing before the scorpion of cold adamant, did genuflect before it. Then he placed his hands within his voluminous robes and pulled out two blazing jewels of crimson, the size of lark's eggs. Of these radiant jewels it is said that within their ruby depths Shalla Bey had deposited all the putrescent evil festering in his heart: all the necromantic knowledge he had obtained down the centuries: all the secrets and forbidden lore of necromancy and the black arts. In short, the sum total of his corrupt and evil knowledge and the secret of his sorcerous longevity.

"It is also said, (but only Zallah is all knowing) that Shalla Bey bethought him to return from the dark vales of the Night Eternal; the Death Realm of Shaizan, and lay claim to the Eyes of the Scorpion and all the vile knowledge contained therein and so he placed the sanguine jewels deep inside the horned skull of a great demon and this he situated at the feet of the scorpion, and it is related that a glow emanated from the sockets and washed the necromancer with twin beams of crimson light and it was as if the evil mage was bathed in blood.

"Shalla Bey then knelt before the eidolon which was the manifestation of Girtab, the Scorpion God and bowed down, kissing the ground between his hands. As he did so, he softly whispered arcane words of magic and the great tail of carven adamant quivered for a moment and then lashed forward fast as a striking cobra, flicking putrid venom as it did so. The wicked scimitar-like sting plunged into the exposed back of Shalla Bey, its poison tip bursting through his emaciated chest and then withdrew, and all in the blink of an eye. Shalla Bey, it is told, gave one sigh as if of extreme pleasure or contentment and his lifeless body slid slowly to the temple floor.

"With the death of the necromancer his undead servitors collapsed wherever they toiled, nothing more than withered dust and dry bones which provided scant provender for the ever ravenous ghuls.

"Since that day, none has visited the necropolis of Khanazur, for there were no conjurings to lure the unwary through its crumbling gates. It remains a city of emaciated ghuls, shunned and cursed by Zallah and there the jewels sit, guarded by the Scorpion God and those ghuls that remain, awaiting the return of the necromancer."

"A fine story Jamal. Worthy of Shazrazar herself!" Sanjar laughed as the group fell to bickering; arguing the merits of Jamal's story.

3. The Geas of Zarallu

I stood a while pondering the strange tale I had overheard, my eyes straying towards the menacing city crouching in the desert gloom like some sleeping genie. My conjectures were interrupted however by the subtle rustling of silks and in an instant my scimitar was in my hand as I looked toward the tent. There I saw an emaciated and claw-like hand extended from the tent folds gesturing for me to enter the pavilion.

That Zarallu should summon me thus was a great astonishment and a strange thing to me, for I had not heard the necromancer make utterance since my appointment as his guard. Indeed since embarking upon this quest I had only actually beheld the sorcerer on a single occasion, and that most recently, for he rarely left his sable shrouded carriage while his pavilion was erected by four brutish creatures that stooped and shambled like great apes and communicated in coarse grunts.

How and when Zarallu left his carriage to enter the tent I did not know. It was but once, as I have related, that I observed him and that was as we ascended a sand dune and first beheld the decaying necropolis. His cowled head was thrust from the black drapes of his carriage and, though I could not see his visage I could discern the glitter of his eyes and it seemed to me that he had regarded me intently for a moment and then, with a fleeting glance at the distant city he had withdrawn once more into the grasping shadows.

I turned my mind from these musings and pulled aside the hangings covering the entranceway to the necro-mancer's pavilion and entered. I found myself in a pungent gloom, heavy with the dark aromas of the yellow lotus and rare perfumes and spices. I stood in a large area, curtained at every wall and furnished with burning braziers.

One far section of the pavilion was in shadow and there I descried, upon a twisted chair of sculpted onyx, the vague form of Zarallu. He lolled upon the chair, wrapped in voluminous folds of black cloth. Again his face I could not see, save for the hard glittering of his purple eyes, for the large hood threw it into deep shadow. Once more he gestured to me to approach. I moved nearer and became aware of a noxious stench underpinning the pungent and aromatic spices.

Then Zarallu gestured weirdly and I detected soft whisperings, like the scales of a snake rasping against stone. A curious sensation began to overwhelm me and I considered the notion that the fumes redolent within the pavilion were powerful narcotic drugs. Concurrent with the cessation of the sibilant whispering I found myself unable to move a single muscle of my body. It was as if I were bound by the silken strands of Ajazib the spider god. No matter how much effort I expended in an attempt to move I could not.

Then the voice of Zarallu rose in pitch and volume: "Harken then to your geas, O Zalim!" spake Zarallu sonorously. "Your geas shall be that you shall go from this

tent and enter Khanazur. There you shall make your way to the Temple of the Scorpion that lies at the heart of that necropolis. You shall penetrate the temple and seek out the twin jewels known as The Eyes of the Scorpion, which repose within. These you shall return to me forthwith." As Zarallu spoke I again felt a tingling sensation in all my limbs. "You shall be permitted to retain your scimitar, for, be assured, it shall be needed, for the jewels are guarded 'gainst the larcenous intent of fools who know not their worth."

At this, Zarallu's withered hand groped within his robes and pulled forth an amulet upon a leather thong. "Beware the Lord of the Ghuls, for he guards the city jealously and will prize your warm flesh, finding it a repast most succulent. Take this talisman, which shall offer protection from the ghuls, for the lord shall recognize it and fear it as shall his minions."

I took the object from Zarallu and recoiled with disgust as I beheld it was the mummified paw of a ghul, the wrist being set in a silver band by which it was attached to the leather thong.

Against my will I found my hands reaching upwards and tying the loathsome amulet about my neck. The paw fell heavily to hang at my breast.

The necromancer's uncanny eyes glittered strangely as he gestured for me to exit the pavilion.

"Be gone, manikin of my desire, fulfil your geas if you would have me cut your strings." I strained mightily to draw my blade and strike Zarallu's head from his wizened torso but it was as if I were paralyzed. For several moments I exerted all my considerable strength and willpower in this wise only to hear Zarallu laughing with amused contempt the while. Finally I desisted and found myself walking from the pavilion, though I had made no conscious decision to do so. As I left the confines of that claustrophobic tent, I felt the night winds upon my face and turned, again against my conscious will, toward the looming necropolis. As I began to walk I found that I could make no progress other than in the direction of that loathsome municipality. It came to me then that Jamal's tale, which I had thought naught but campfire bravado, might hold more than a grain of truth. So, resigning myself to my uncertain fate, I strode purposefully towards the decaying gates of Khanazur.

4. Lord of the Ghuls

And so it was that, by the coruscating light of the rising

moon, I crossed the desert sands and entered the brooding necropolis. The ruined streets and avenues at first seemed desolate and deserted but soon I perceived vague forms moving amid the shadows, keeping pace with me as I strode deeper into the city. Then, as I entered a great plaza these forms left the shadows and approached me. I felt a shiver of fear as I realized they were ghuls. They flocked about me, their rank pelts tainting the night breeze with their carrion stench. They licked their slavering muzzles as they contemplated me, their canine noises wrinkling as they sniffed the aroma of living flesh. But not one drew near and I realized the power of Zarallu's morbid talisman. It had been a long while since living flesh stalked these avenues of death however and, despite the power of the severed paw, they loped at my heels like beaten curs, their ravenous eyes gleaming.

At length, I came upon the steps of a once splendid palace and there stopped. I surveyed the noisome throng of ghuls that stood or squatted about me, noting their dripping jowls and starving eyes. Then I heard a disturbance emanating from the palace and turning I descried, coming from within the decaying building, loping through the shattered doorway, a ghul of impressive stature, whose yellow fangs glistened with saliva and whose amber eyes gleamed with evil. I understood that this fearsome creature was the Lord of the Ghuls so I fixed my gaze upon the terrible creature and smiled.

Putting my left hand upon the severed paw I lifted it and spoke: "I seek the Temple of the Scorpion." I said, my eyes still staring into those orbs of lambent amber flame.

"Many have sought the temple, O man, and all have

failed," the ghul Lord rejoined, "are you not fearful of the way?"

"I have neither fear nor concern, vile one," spake I.

"Verily you are a brave man or a fool," said the Lord, incensed at my insult. "But I perceive that you are neither, for you are merely the unwitting instrument of some malign necromancer who desires the Eyes of the Scorpion for himself."

Despite the geas that had been laid upon me, still I did feel the sting to my pride that the rank creature had sought to inflict.

"Persist in obstructing my way carrion spawn and verily you will soon comprehend which of us is the fool," said I through gritted teeth taking a step toward the verminous ghul lord.

"So be it," said the Lord, backing away with a low growl, "You may proceed. But know this: I shall have retribution for the insult you have tendered me. Be it in the blackened catacombs below or upon moonlit desert sands, you shall feel my ravening teeth at your throat and of a certainty I shall feast upon the tender meat of your body!"

"Show me where lies the temple!" I commanded.

The ghul's gaze flickered from mine to the talisman and for a moment I thought hate and hunger might overwhelm the potent sorceries of Zarallu, but it was not so. Instead, the thing simply indicated the direction I had to go and I noticed with a shiver of disgust that its arm ended at the wrist. I knew then the origin of the foul object about my throat. With this maimed limb the ghul gestured toward a great black dome that stood at the heart of the necropolis and I recognized the Temple of the Scorpion from the tale of Jamal. It was there that the objects of my unwilling quest lay

As I moved away from the pack of slavering ghuls I did note that none made to follow me and the thought occurred to me that perchance it was their fear of the domed building rather than the potency of Zarallu's talisman that held them thus.

I walked towards the great dome, onward into the depths of this unwholesome municipality, making my cautious way through the perpetual silence of the stagnant necropolis. And such was the emptiness and constant quiet of this place, that my mind entertained many thoughts of intense strangeness, for at times my body would move in directions contrary to mine intentions, and this was most unsettling. Within myself I wrestled with the necromancer's geas, but his power was strong and I could not assert my will, unless my intentions were in accord with that of Zarallu's. Thus I strode through the shattered avenues, past broken tombs and sepulchres, a mere plaything of the necromancer.

The oppressive solitude came close to overwhelming my spirit and despair fed like a parasite upon my will and it seemed like a million years of silence pressed down upon me as I walked. Then I stood before the temple of The Scorpion God. The great shadowed dome loomed before me, supported by its pillars of mighty girth and great height. Upward they stretched, carved of black basalt until surmounted by the incredible dome of dark jade and ebony. Before me a flight of seven low stairs led upward between two of these titanic pillars to arrive at a great entranceway whose ebony doors, filigreed with tarnished silver, hung torn and ruined from great buckled hinges. Propelled by the evil geas, I ascended the steps and walked through the shattered doors, pondering on what mighty force could have broken and twisted them thus. The merchant's tale came unbidden to my mind and I wondered again at the veracity of his story. Shrugging, I passed under the archway and walked into the cool dark.

5.Tendrils of Death

I had entered a vast circular chamber, barren of features and with no other exit. The ceiling was lost in shadowed gloom but I surmised it to be nothing less than the interior of the great dome. In the centre of the cavernous room was the pit. It too was circular in dimension and no less than fifty paces in diameter. As to its depth I could make no accurate conjecture, for it plunged deep into brooding darkness. I noticed a set of stone steps descending about the wall of the pit deep into its interior.

Against my will, the insidious compulsion of the geas urged me onwards and I knew that I must venture down into this inky well of darkness. I placed my foot upon the first step and began my descent.

I knew not what awaited me at the bottom of the pit, and this weighed heavy upon my heart, for without a doubt I was Zarallu's plaything. But I did resolve that if I survived my present predicament, I would see that he would regret his arrogance in placing this geas upon me, for I would return to slay the vile necromancer and cut out his black, infected heart.

Slowly I made my descent of the stone stairway that twisted about the walls of the shaft. The steps seemed to be cut for a larger stride than that of a man and I wondered what purpose the pit served. Mayhap it was a doorway to the abode of Jinn and Demon, or the entranceway to the fabled realm of The Night Eternal where the ghuls did rule from their rotting charnel thrones. Yet still I descended, slave to Zarallu's vile will.

I progressed slowly and cautiously, lest a careless slip plunge me into the abyss, for about me the darkness was absolute. I walked with my left hand ever against the wall for guidance feeling every step tentatively. How long I descended thus I cannot say but I continued to creep downwards at a slow, torturous pace. Then it felt to me that the air grew warmer and soon a hot, dry breeze could be felt issuing from below. With this, I realized that a faint illumination was also visible beneath me, which increased as I descended. I could now see the uneven steps at my feet and in a short time I finally beheld the floor of the pit. Within moments, I had reached the last step. I saw then that the illumination, which had guided my final descent, sprang from vile fungi that grew in profusion on the cavern floor. Pallid ropy tendrils as thick as palm trees and tall as a man grew in a tangled forest of twisted limbs. The flesh of these obscene growths was luminescent, though the weak rose coloured light did not travel far, which explained why I had not been aware of it from the rim of the pit above. And here I did pause to wonder how deep was this pit, for I had descended for a great while as my aching limbs testified.

As I drew nearer the growths, I saw that each tendril was veined and it was blood coursing within these huge, knotted arteries that caused the glow to be tainted with crimson. As I watched, I saw that the tendrils swayed and pulsed with the passing of the thick, crimson fluid. I wondered what heart pumped the blood through those vile growths when suddenly I knew apprehension and disgust as the movement of the tendrils became livelier the closer I approached them. Then, as they leaned in my direction, I perceived that the end of each growth terminated in a small crimson flower of five small petals in the shape of a star. At the centre of the star, a pair of pink, fleshy jaws, like the soft lips of a lamia, rippled as if in anticipation.

Before me, a narrow, twisting path led through the glowing forest of swaying flesh but I dared not enter for fear that these parasitic plants would feast upon my own blood. And I knew this to be a surety for I noticed that at the base of many of these obscene growths there were piles of white, crumbling bones, and I saw that these were the charnel remains of ghuls, earlier victims of the loathsome plants.

I turned about and looked at the stairway I had so recently descended. Looking up, I yearned to retrace my steps but the geas laid upon me by Zarallu made that impossible. Rather would I brave the deadly perils of the vampire growths than return to the open air such was the quality of his terrible magic.

It was then that I felt a curious sensation upon my shoulder, as of the soft fingers of a perfumed concubine. These unseen fingers probed sensuously, caressing the flesh of my neck seductively. Then a dread realization came to me and in horror I turned and in one motion ripped the tendril from my body and drew my gleaming scimitar. The forest of fungi was indeed alive!

A dreadful hissing sound filled the air as above and about me the lashing tendrils writhed and groped. Blood flowed freely from several small puncture wounds upon my neck and shoulder and it was a surety that the foul plant-things scented the warm fluid, for their motions became most frantic. More tendrils snaked towards me, and two began to twine about my thighs, their immense coiled power nearly sweeping me from my feet. I swung my sword in a shining arc and severed the coils, which were almost as thick as the limbs they held. The ropy tendrils fell to the sand, leaking blood and a foul smelling yellow ichor that steamed as it stained the ground. More tendrils made to entrap me as I worked my sword in such manner so as to sever each swaying limb as it took hold of my body. Unarmed, I would have been slain within moments; even so I was swiftly losing strength from the exertion of my battle and the loss of blood from the wounds inflicted by the thirsting limbs. I felt pressure about my legs and looked down and realized with mounting horror that the severed coils were wriggling towards me and climbing snake-like up my legs.

I screamed "Zallah guide me!" and surged forward, sweeping my scimitar about me mightily, sending tendrils, blood, and ichor arcing through the air in all directions. I fought with the sure knowledge that the battle must end soon, else my death was certain.

I was still struggling when at last it came to me that the attack was over. The ensanguined pieces upon the sand were slithering away leaving sticky trails of gore as they went. Then I perceived with satisfaction that the plants sought to avoid me as I moved. It was as if all were aware of the danger I represented and that, by some manner, they now sensed that I was not a morsel they could overpower with ease and so were turning away in search of easier prey. It was a surety their usual victims were not as hard to kill as I!

If the things had eyes to see, I must have presented a savage and terrible sight: wild-eyed and bloodstained, my blade, dripping mingled gore and ichor, gripped tightly in a bloodied fist.

It was then as I regained my breath, that I saw, concealed within the shadows beneath the stairway I had descended, a small entranceway in the side of the pit. It was black as a Houri's heart but I was compelled to enter the unknown darkness for it seemed my only choice…if indeed it was choice rather than the malicious guiding hand of Zarallu. If I were indeed a puppet of the necromancer then I would make his quest mine and secure The Eyes of the Scorpion. Then…when the geas was lifted…then would I deal with Zarallu!

Turning my back on the forest of twitching horrors I entered the tunnel, plunging once more into the unknown.

6. The Scorpion God

The passage I had entered was narrow, for in the darkness I had stretched out my arms on either side and felt the dry stone of the irregular walls. Slowly I made my way forward, guided by touch alone. My progress was of necessity slow, for I had to be wary of a sudden pit or chasm that might lay unseen in the floor before me. Thus, I tested every step I took tentatively before moving forward. It was much the same manner as I had descended the stairs into the pit and truly it was a method I had become accustomed to since entering this realm of darkness.

After travelling thus for many minutes I observed a radiance before me. Fearful that it might signal another grove of parasitic flesh-things, I proceeded with utmost caution until there was sufficient light that I no longer needed to use my limbs for guidance.

It was with some relief that I soon discovered that

the light was emanating from fluorescent fungi which grew upon the walls of the tunnel and so, still with some caution, I continued upon my way. On either side of me dark openings yawned, but, enslaved by the geas that compelled me, I steadfastly traversed the main corridor until from one of the passageways I heard the mournful sounds of a child weeping. I hesitated, fighting the pull of the geas, then, from yet another of the openings issued the plaintive cries of a woman in distress. My hesitation was my salvation for it came to me that it was most unlikely that a living child or a woman would be trapped beneath a city dead for uncounted centuries. Then, Zarallu's spell reasserted itself and ignoring the sounds, I moved on.

A third branching I also disregarded and continued on the path before me for I saw that a few paces ahead it was obscured by a dark velvet curtain that hung from brass rings in the stone ceiling concealing what lay beyond.

Drawing the curtain aside, I stepped beyond the threshold and into a large and lofty chamber. The high ceiling was wreathed in shadows and festooned with tattered cobwebs. Crumbling tapestries adorned the walls; rotting carpets lay strewn upon the uneven flags and broken furniture lay scattered everywhere.

In the centre of the chamber there stood a plinth of black adamant, veined with red, which rose to waist height. Upon it was a carven statue, also of black adamant and I shuddered at its aspect. It was a scorpion; cunningly moulded from the ebon stone and the unknown sculptor had imbued it with a malefic aura that chilled my very soul. It was twice the height of a man and its wicked sting curved over its body and terminated just above the monster's head. In every aspect save in size, it resembled the creature upon which it had been fashioned and in the uncertain light it seemed to me most lifelike. The statue stood rampant over a skull, though surely it was the skull of a demon for the thing was of a great size. Deep within the eye sockets of this skull something sanguine glistened, catching the light and reflecting it in crimson shards. I drew closer and to my astonishment beheld within the skull two marvellous rubies that pulsed with a deep crimson. These, I knew, must be the Eyes of the Scorpion and the objects of my unwilling quest. It occurred to me then that the tale of Jamal had possibly been correct in every detail save a slight exaggeration of the dimensions of the scorpion idol.

Though I knew dread and apprehension at the fearful scene before me, still I was compelled by the geas laid upon me by Zarallu and so it was that I placed my left hand into the left eye socket of the demon skull and made to withdraw the fantastic jewels. As I did so, my fingers took on a florid scarlet glow as the light of the scintillating rubies washed over them. I had begun to admire the singular effect when I felt a sharp pain lance my hand and with a gasp of shock and surprise withdrew it from the cache and, looking closely, saw that there was a small wound in the flesh between thumb and forefinger. It was an angry red that quickly began to swell and I praised Zallah and the seven gods that I had used my left hand to explore the skull instead of my sword hand. As I nursed my wound I saw a small black shape scuttle from between the gaping jaws of the demon skull and fall to the floor. Looking down, I saw with alarm that it was a scorpion, a living reflection of the abhorrent idol. Its night black body was marked upon the back with a crimson star and I realized with dread that the sting of the red scorpion meant a slow, agonizing death!

*   *   *

As the vile creature scuttled away across the floor, I sat myself down; my back against the cavern wall, for even the geas could not impel me further. The jade eyes of the Scorpion God seemed to gaze down upon me mockingly.

My hand was now swollen to twice its normal size and was throbbing with a burning pain that was slowly spreading up my arm, turning the engorged flesh an angry purple.

Within minutes, an uncontrollable shaking and an intense fever gripped me. Was I to die here, alone and forgotten brought down by a lowly scorpion?

A lethargy began to overwhelm me.

I closed my eyes and knew madness…

I was in a maelstrom of vivid nightmare. Coruscating colours swirled past my eyes and a gibbering laughter echoed about me as my head was flooded with a tide of insanity.

I stood upon a crimson plain, the sands of which stretched to every horizon and every red grain was a dried drop of human blood. A breeze brushed my face, the stolen breath of a million souls, their last gasps before they were claimed by oblivion. Great bone edifices writhed and twisted upwards from the ruddy sand and tore at the pallid grey skies. Leprous, ochre-hued, multi-legged insects scuttled with rattling noises over the charnel artifacts. Their eyes shone like dark jewels and their soulless gazes were fixed upon me.

Again the insane, gleeful laughter.

There, before his obsidian throne, in a cavern of dancing flame stood Girtab, the Scorpion God, in all his evil magnificence. The dead and dying surrounded him; naked humans, heaped in untidy piles. Some were kissed by the relentless fires and writhed in mortal agony, their still living flesh bubbling and melting in the heat, others were blackened and charred and gave off a thick noxious smoke which choked my lungs. Screams and confusion reigned all around. I crouched, trembling with fear as the Scorpion God reached out a dripping claw, crimson with the blood of the slain and gestured. All about me flames leaped upward and engulfed me. The god laughed as I screamed!

An undulating desert of bleached and shattered bone.

Suddenly there came to view a whole army of grotesque beasts. I could hardly believe the awful sight I looked upon. There were hundreds of them, black and sinful, snarling and terrible. The grotesque stench of putrefied flesh filled all the air, causing me to retch horribly. They stumbled towards me, these beasts of nightmare, their misshapen snouts quivering, their lambent eyes glaring, their reeking pelts dripping. I tried to flee but my muscles were numb. Then, as one, the Army of Night knelt in worship before me…

Grey mists swirled about me.

Clammy tendrils caressed the skin of my face.

I stood upon a pinnacle of shattered rock that rose from a sea of swirling mist. Upon a similar height stood another figure regarding me with glowing scarlet eyes. His raiment was black and about his shoulders hung a black cloak. Within the sea of fog I could discern pale shapes that moved mysteriously through the rolling clouds. Though vague and indistinct, they were somehow threatening and obscene.

They were not human.

Occasionally I would glimpse a fragile white face among the many, contorted in exquisite agony, with large expressive almond eyes staring into mine, imploring me with their looks. I felt I could free them from their eternal tortures if it was my wish, but I chose not to do so, for I thrived on their suffering and fed on their ceaseless agony. I saw the black figure smile…

*   *   *

I was again in the cavern before the scorpion idol, my back against the chamber wall. My fever had passed and the swelling in my hand and arm had receded. My mind still reeled from the visions I had beheld. I could not explain their meaning, if indeed any existed, nor could I explain having recovered from what I believed to be a certain death. Lifting my arm to examine it more carefully, I saw that there was a small puncture wound over that of the scorpion sting and from it, a teardrop of blood welled free. I looked to my side and saw a blackened, shrivelled plant, similar to those that grew in the vampire forest, though of much diminished proportion, and realized that by some irony, the scorpion's poison had saved my life.

It had chanced that after being stung by the creature, I had collapsed next to the loathsome plant, which had sensed the presence of blood and fastened itself onto my puncture wound. It had then begun to greedily feed, drawing the poison into itself with my blood. The result was that its instinctive action had saved my life at the cost of its own. Shakily, I regained my feet and with one last doubtful gaze into the hollow, mocking eyes of the idol, I carefully withdrew the two gleaming rubies from within the skull and placed them inside my pouch.

7. Attack of the Ghuls

I turned and passed again through the curtains and by the eerie fungal illumination slowly made my way back up the tunnel. After a time I noticed that the floor was scattered with charnel filth. As I had not discerned its presence during my descent, I guessed that I had perchance taken a wrong turn at some point. As bones cracked sharply beneath my sandals, It came to me that they likely indicated the lurking presence of ghuls. With mounting concern, I quickened my pace because, though I was armed with a scimitar and protected by the talisman given me by Zarallu, I did not relish a meeting with a pack of the creatures in those gloomy tunnels. Hoping that the ascending floor meant eventual release from the bowels of the palace, I hurried upwards and in my haste sent many bones scattering with sharp echoes that bounced along the tunnel walls.

Then I heard something.

I stopped momentarily in my ascent and listened. Behind me, I could faintly discern sounds of pursuit for I could hear a weird snuffling and *sniffing* as though the creatures were seeking my scent. Then, a bloodcurdling howl reverberated upwards from below and I realized with dismay that I had been discovered.

Instinctively, my hand sought the talisman about my neck; Zarallu's gift to protect me from the bloodthirsty ghuls and I realized with a thrill of horror that it was not there. I had lost it! No doubt it had fallen from my neck as I had writhed in tortured agony in the chamber of the Scorpion God. And there, of a surety, it still lay.

Hurriedly, I resumed my progress, running where I could, praising Zallah for the illumination, for without it I surely would have been slain before ever I reached safety.

Behind me, the sounds of pursuit were growing. A gruesome barking and whining accompanied the slap of paws upon stone.

In moments, the things would be upon me. I stopped, resolving to stand my ground and meet these carrion creatures face to face rather than have them drag me down while on the run. I found good footing among the flagstones, drew my scimitar, and awaited the first glimpse of my pursuers.

It was not long in coming. The pack of mangy, emaciated beasts scrabbled into view, their lambent eyes gleaming with hunger and anticipation. Suddenly, they came to a halt, for they were used to their prey running in fear but I stood tense and prepared, ready to die for, if this was to be my final battle it was my intention to take as many of the vile things with me as I could.

Slowly, warily, the ghuls began to advance and deciding not to wait their pleasure, I lunged at the foremost, slashing at its neck, and opening the throat below the slavering muzzle. It collapsed in a tangle of arms and legs and expired in a fountain of crimson gore but of this I took little heed as, striking again, I reduced the pack by another member.

A ghul with a scabrous pelt, weeping with open sores, snarled and lunged at me, but his movements were slow and clumsy. He managed to parry my first wild thrust with his length of bone and then tried to stab at me with the sharpened end, but missed as I moved rapidly aside. Recovering I sent the tip of my sword between its jaws and killed it.

Still the ghuls pressed forward, some clutching charnel remains as clubs others with bones in their hands, splintered or sharpened to wicked points. But, hampered by the narrowness of the tunnel, they could not bring their full numbers to bear.

At my feet, the dead were piling high and those still living were forced to scramble over the corpses of their companions to reach me. My blood coursed through my veins like fire and I knew exultation beyond measure as I slew the foul creatures. All my frustrations and fears knew release as I took life after life. Ah, if only I could slay Zarallu as easily!

Finally, I saw that before me stood one final beast, but one of mighty size and formidable aspect. I recognized it as the Lord of the Ghuls! In its long fingered paw it held a rusted sword, no doubt thieved from the chamber of the Scorpion God, for I had seen similar weaponry there. Its lambent eyes burned with hate and hunger and I saw with horror that about its neck hung the talisman!

"So, it seems we meet again, O man," growled the thing as it swayed before me.

"If you would taste of my flesh eater of carrion, then here I stand!" I taunted.

As I guessed, my words enraged the thing and with a piercing howl, it threw caution aside and came at me, sword held high for a killing stroke. Many men would have stood transfixed by that abominable scream and been slain instantly but the battle madness was still upon me and I sprang to meet the creature in mid-stride. Diving low under the thing's clumsy swing, my blade opened the flesh beneath its ribs as I continued past. The creature was forced to drop its weapon and, clutching its side, lunged at me again, its fangs bared and aimed at my throat. But I had no intention of allowing those yellowed teeth to sink in my flesh! Again, I avoided its charge and plunged my sword deep into its exposed chest, cleaving its blackened heart.

With the demise of the Lord of Ghuls, the madness abated and I was consumed with exhaustion. For a moment I stood and gazed upon the pile of tangled corpses, then I made to examine what wounds I had sustained and perceived that there were none to cause me great concern, for all were slight, and most of the blood that caked my skin was ghul blood. The many hours I had spent learning swordplay under the tutelage of the legendary Zinbar had stood me in good stead, for I was accounted the greatest swordsman in all Sharador.

Choosing to leave the disgusting talisman on the gory chest of the ghul Lord I turned and ascended the last few remaining feet of the tunnel, which finally opened out upon a balcony from which a broad stairway descended to the dusty street below. Overhead, the early morning stars twinkled in a familiar sky and below stood the shattered gates of the city from which I had entered hours before. With the geas that had been cast upon me finally in accord with my own desires, I exited Khanazur and prepared to seek out my master, the unscrupulous Zarallu!

*   *   *

As I passed the city's gates, dawn began to redden the

eastern horizon. I had spent the entire night within the Temple of the Scorpion! Of ghuls and other foul creatures of the night there was no sign and I ventured to guess that it was likely the rays of the rising sun that kept them at bay rather than fear of my sword. But I allowed myself little time to ponder the situation as ahead, I noticed to my dismay, that the caravan of Ali Hassan was no longer encamped in the dunes where it had been the previous evening. All that remained was Zarallu's solitary black pavilion and my horse tethered nearby.

8. Zarallu

Slowly I approached the morbid tent and as I neared it the curtains in the entranceway were pulled aside by a skeletal hand and in a moment the ebon clad figure of Zarallu stood before me. Still ensorcelled, I halted before him and attempted to peer into the deep shadow inside his cowl, but I failed to make out his face or discern the glitter of his purple eyes. Zarallu stood, somewhat shakily I fancied, and I noted that in stature, he stood at least a head shorter than I. Unable to reconcile this wasted personage to the figure I had seen stalking the necropolis of Zarathis, I wondered if some disease or malaise had seized him in its grip. Even as I considered, a hand slowly lifted and threw back the concealing cowl from about Zarallu's head.

I stepped back a pace in horror and disgust at what was revealed. I cannot say what I had thought to see but of a surety it was not the horribly mottled skin; the strangely elongated skull and the suppurating wounds that constituted the necromancer's head and face. And though that face possessed a mouth and nose after a fashion, there were no eyes. Instead, I found myself staring into a pair of empty sockets, both weeping tears of gelid blood.

And then, worst of all, Zarallu smiled!

As I stood transfixed in horror, my hand moved of its own accord. Reaching into the pouch at my side, it withdrew the crimson jewels I had taken from the temple and offered them to Zarallu.

The necromancer reached out with a fist that was caked in blood and when the fingers opened, two crimson orbs fell to the sand. Not rubies as I thought at first. Nay! They were Zarallu's eyes, plucked from his own deformed skull! The mirthless grin that creased his face was terrible to behold and was followed by a rattling laugh that crawled out of his withered throat.

Then, as I looked on, still under his spell, he took the proffered rubies in his ensanguined hand and placed them in his empty eye sockets.

"At last!" he shouted in triumph. "The dark secrets of Shalla Bey shall be mine! I shall rule Sharador and my every whim shall be law!"

Then Zarallu's expression changed to that of puzzlement.

"No!" screamed the sorcerer, raising his hands to his tormented face. "No!

Even as I watched, Zarallu began to twitch and shake, his robes filling out in a grotesque fashion even as his stature increased. And then did the necromancer drink deeply from the cup of despair as he realized the nature of the doom that had overcome him.

One that became clear to myself as well. The potentate known as Shalla Bey had poured his very life essence into the shimmering jewels awaiting this very day and that essence was now exerting its will over the form of Zarallu, consuming his very spirit to give the ancient necromancer life and form. Shalla Bey was returning! Returning to live for another thousand years!

Even as I watched and conjectured, Zarallu continued to change. Already he stood two heads taller than I and lank, white hair began to sprout from his warping skull.

Then, in the midst of the transformation, when the body before me was neither Zarallu nor truly that of Shalla Bey, the geas that had been laid upon me lifted and suiting action to thought, I wasted little time in lopping the monstrous head from the quaking shoulders.

It flew through the morning air to land with a thump upon the desert sand, there to stare up at me, frozen in a horrible look that captured the features of both Zarallu and Shalla Bey!

Disgusted at the whole turn of affairs, I made my way to my horse and prepared to depart that cursed ground. Mounted, I took one last glance at the remains of my former master and there I saw twin columns of smoke rising from the darkened sockets of the severed head. In them, the crimson gleam had faded and I knew the Eyes of Scorpion were no more.

Contemplating the folly of vanity and the lust for power, I turned away and began the long journey back toward the marbled walls of Sharador.

THE FLIGHT OF THE TICO
Frederick J. Mayer

"Wake-up! Had this dream stopped?..." click.

With a morphean thanatoid mind shroud temporarily removed and a simple yawn, Dr. Koh Rei-am turned the machine off while reflecting upon how much he had always enjoyed listening to the old Lizard King's recordings, especially, that epic piece "The Celebration of the Lizard." Once a source of childhood pleasure, now, a source of sanity and just a plain means of staying awake and alive.

The now long dead Lizard King all dressed in ebony black leather was, in a strange way, considered an "ancestral poet" to Dr. Koh's people (once known originally as the "Tcho Tcho") because that royal entity's mordent blending of morphemics so captured the Tcho conceptional tongue of yore...before the long forgotten trek and the fleshy, among other ways, integration with the present "Korean" stock of Jeju-do (or Cheju Island).

The slithering subtle pain of Kundalini serpent stylised strides up and down Koh's's diminutive body structure suddenly re-struck its focused fangs stingingly back into his already selvage stripped brain, singingly mordant into his synaptic nervous system with such splitting, spitting pain awareness once more was on now not then.

"Now. Now? Now! Where am I and where is now?" Koh's own Self re-adjusted physically itself. "Oh, yes, sitting inside the Starship Tico. Sitting...the lower part of my anatomy has been knifed, diced, mashed and meshed with the lightly metallic front font console board. How long I have been in such an intimate relationship I really am not sure nor care...seems only fair considering some members of my progenitors' extended modern group was responsible for its successful construction and design by Daewoo, Korea's leading manufacturer of such component parts and moving vehicles...aaah, genius on their part to integrate the toilet system into the overall seating situation."

Dr. Koh continued his slow, weary spoken aloud thoughts to the confines of the ship, "We have, it seems, always been good with our highly creative minds and hands. Our slightly longer, slenderer than normal fingers and hard nails, naturally artistic some have said of people generally constructed that way, seemed customized for such endeavours. Metallurgy has been said to have originated somewhere in South-East Asia. I would hardly be so bold to claim my true ancestors had a part in it then, though, our roots are "Asian" and we have for eons occupied parts of that terrain. Yet, family legends have us being forever excelling in "carving" and metal work.

Daewoo even named my country's (currently referred to as Korea) first truly compact cars, around the early 1990's, after my "tribe," though they didn't realize it (and, us in the giant firm making sure the Romanised lettering was a bit altered). The Korean business conglomerate gave the honour of naming that highly test successful little mode of transportation to its inventive engineers - highly unusual, but they were "seniors" within the company. Thus, the "Tico" was born. So what if the original Tico eventually became the national butt of all automobile jokes, the car worked and achieved its goals ...and this mini-ship's name comes from that first breakthrough super-compact vehicle on four wheels."

"Some of those attempts at humour still abound," Koh continued under the decaying light, shimmering burnt golden hue of the craft. "How does one stop a runaway Tico? Put a wad of some freshly chewed gum on the road just in front of it...ok, ha ha...there were some valid reasons for the jabs, or so I'm told...the petite Tico was an extremely light car and a good, solid wind, as it is known to exist in Korea, actually could blow it across parts of an expressway. In fact, I think upon it again, now, that that is what probably caused the current predicament of this vessel. We were meant to land on the dry, lovely blood-coloured Mars...this is not that planet, I was brought onto this threesome team because of my extensive knowledge of such things (my kin were always highly tuned to the celestial bodies and such)...not sure what wind-like occurrence happened, solar flare or something, nor...do I understand how we got here...don't recall anything... anything like a worm-hole and their transporting ilk...bouncing, shaking, dancingly were we all...suddenly, slipping, ejaculating into this pale pearly soiled soil upon some more solidified...wham bam slammed damned point first into this place."

Koh's mouth kept moving, "Where is now? Where am...perhaps, 'where' is outside, where this miniaturised space carrier of three now resides. I remember James, James Wade Amberville, our pilot and fearless leader, James's words coming back over the Tico's sound system, through my aural systems...'strange place, all silent and desolate...can't describe, sedge, ship in boggy, no gummy ground, substance all around, outgrowths fling themselves backwards, forwards, other ways, so...but, no wind, fauna...or flora really...some small stagnant pools born of bulbous drippings from filaments, like bulbochaete, not green, chaet, chaite, chaeta, chaetae, chaetae chaetae... styxian nourished growth...everywhere, enfold overhead, canopy of miasmic...I swear guardian spirit...unholy."

Unholy. Dr. Koh had heard that disgusting term so often applied to those he was descended from. Dark wisps of nostalgia carried him further into the caverns of memory, back where there's never any pain. At the knees of his great grandmamma Rei and ever so bony, no, there were strong, tawny muscles on that ancient tiny skeletal structure of hers. They all said he really was "her" child.

She told him that thousands of years ago the Tcho Tcho moved out of central Asia, some ended up in what is now called Myanmar. Koh's clan, the "Rei," slowly moved down through the mountainous regions onto the Korean peninsula. The holy Lama of legend, Yian-ho, went with the Indo-Chinese (or they with him) grouping, though, the Rei kept their ever-consummating Queen. They have always had a female centric society (some told Rei-am that great grand would have been a queen in another age, in fact, the great Yian-ho himself gave the Queen one of the exceptionally few written copies of their holy text, "Gumi-gan-ok Chaek" or "The Book of Cracked Jade").

Down and up through the steep mountainous landscape of the peninsula they travelled with Dr. Koh's predecessors becoming quite adapted to mountain living, as opposed to the more jungle mode of the Tcho Tcho people who wound their way into the deeper vert and humid regions of Asia. Great grand Rei told how much of Korea's shrouded mystical past and superstitious beliefs have their origins set in encounters with his people. "Those so called 'Spirit Poles' of Koreans...the ones used to protect their local villages and, usually, set just outside their gathering of homes," she grins, revealing a severely gapped teeth arrangement that were highly efficient, and continues the tale, "Ha, they were originally what we erected, out of wood, trees actually, as temporary holy statues to our gods...the glorious male and female twins Lloigor and Zhar! Ever notice those totem poles are always in pairs? And, 'smiling.'"

These Tcho Tcho people, however, kept moving southward for reasons not even old Rei knew the "why." Eventually, they settled on the volcano created island now called Jeju and lived within the vast numbers of deep subterranean tunnels and caverns mainly centred around Mt Halla, though the tunnels network the entire isle. The lake that formed in the crater of Halla became key to the Tcho Tcho of Jeju (as it became sacred to the forth coming "Koreans") and, as Koh's most elderly of guardians were forever quick to point out, "though beautiful it is without doubt, the place could never match the wonders of the 'Lake of Dread' and its wondrous beyond compare 'Isle of Stars'!" She made Dr. Koh promise to take her to the lake before she died. When questioned why make such an arduous trip, the great Rei's unique eyes flashed open and she calmly stated, "...that is where the plateau of Sung lies and the terrestrial home of our gods," perceiving young Rei-am's equally shaped eyes' request, she added, "they were buried alive under there!"

Alive! The power, filarioid flaring pain surged, exploded inside Dr. Koh's cranium seemingly more powerful than the flare of the rainbow of reds and glowing yellows produced at the lift-off of the Tico's mother ship, the "Phoenix II." Then, his double eyelids snapped wide revealing the doctor's eyes of blazing black coals just heated in a furnace stoked by Hephaestus himself. Through the orifice called a mouth, he mumbled, "Where's soju, that abominable Korean drink, but great at numbing one's mind and soul, when one needs a bottle or two...hmmm Anne?" Anne didn't respond as Dr Koh watched what was left of commander Amberville continue to disintegrate on top of the vessel's forward litten, "James, forever with that unlit cigarette dangling from your lips, now...," Koh grinned continuing to verbalize words into the Tico's enclosed air, "your whole lip dangles as its flesh peals from your all- American jaw bone." Amberville had been plastered on the window ever since he tried to escape as this "planet's" sticky, mephitic acid rain-like downpour surprisingly struck a while back catching him unawares during one of his exploratory treks. He may have been the group's leader and pilot, but, if anything had to do with animal, plant or mineral, James was their go to guy, just as Rei-am was the astro-whatever expert. What was growing out there seemed familiar to the American, but he never would commit to actually declaring "what." "What would you call that ever forward moving thing out there now, James," the Korean-Tcho doctor thought, "it's getting closer ever closer and seems determined on intersecting, on placing the Tico et. al. in its glittering something like huge, extremely lean row of singular of movement teeth. Professor Anne never opted an opinion on the matter.

Professor/Dr. Anne Du Voor was one of those individuals who had an endless list of degrees and Dr. Koh had first met this stout, juicy Western robusty apple shaped woman for the first time when they were both graduate students at Miskatonic University and platonically shared an apartment together. Koh's lacreated brain seeped back into the darkening recesses of his grey matter.

After Rei-am graduated with honours from Korea's top university, Seoul National, his guardians sent him off to the hidden centre of all Tcho Tcho secret and valued knowledge, the city of Alaozar, a place he had been once before when he escorted his great grandmother to the island where the city was located. There he was steeped in all it had to offer - besides having his own copy of their holy book (which he was already thoroughly trained in, language used and all) - Rei-am dived into his natural area of interest: that of other works involved with the vastness and voids of varying extra-terrestrial spaces. Plus, there were such works as the "Ponape Scripture" and "Zanthu Tablets." However, it was made very clear his original people of race did not come from Mu or Lemuria.

Over time, Koh returned to Jeju to be then sent off to gain the outer world's recognition of degrees. Knowledge and foremost the Sciences were important to the Rei branch, who had become, over a lengthy time span, for all practical purposes Koreans in look and acceptance (his line hadn't messed up with the cross breeding as did those idiots the Deep Ones, or so his family informed.) Once in awhile, there were Tcho Tcho-Koreans who needed some dental work and they were always wary of their eyes giving them away...but,

Westerners never could visually separate Asians and Koh's folks were just written off as these odd ball Asians from some place called Jeju a place even Koreans were of a mind that was a bit off the Korean culture wall with their language, female centred society (the island province was the only one, the rest of the country was a typical Confucian male hierarchy), art/statues like the famed island trademark, the phallic, hat wearing "Dol-harubang" or "Stone Grandfather" and the distinctively different from the Korean mainland's folk beliefs and legends. Many have speculated this unusual cultural behaviour and development was due to Jeju belonging more to Oceanian roots or realms. Great grandmother Rei said, "Don't you believe it!"

Koh met up with Du Voor again by meeting her at a Seoul "Open Mic" held in that city's district called Itaewon within a revered old rock club called "Woodstock." The venerable owner Mr. Woo had always supported the expatriate community, especially, the more talented ones, as well as, providing a nifty place to spend time, socialize and have a few brews. Up until then, neither had realized they were both living in Korea and in the country's megatropolis capital. The two quickly renewed their shared tastes in the various and esoteric arts, spending many an hour discussing the finer points of literature, so, in the more "mystical" legends and facts areas, Rei-am had to stop short his sometimes wish to correct Du Voor's vast knowledge on something, least he had to reveal his own source of such information.

February 29th was an important date, other than marking a "Leap Year," because on that day both had been notified they were to be part of the starship Tico's crew (he representing Asia, she Europe and Amberville

North America) and it was the day of the book signing party for Anne's latest book of poetry, "Loves I Bear To You," which was published in the languages of French and English. Anne was a scholarly, but satyr type whose lust for life fit well to her living in the Itaewon-do area, an area that honestly earned its seedy, notorious nightlife reputation. Yet, it did have its more truly arty abodes such as "Abby's Book Nook," where the current tome of Du Voor's work was being officially released in Korea that evening.

Dr. Koh so missed seeing his beloved stars, hidden by day by Seoul's ever present smog and by night, in Itaewon, by the ever present neon lights that turned the darkest night into the brightest day. It wasn't Jeju, but he lived on nearby "Namsan" ("South Mountain") and there he had a peek or two of the jewels of the black ink sky. All he wanted now, "I want to go home."

Having met Anne at the base of the hill where Abby's rested on top, the two headed for the book shop...past the first winding street to their left which was nicknamed "Hooker Hill," for all the "Juicy Bars" that wound their way up that avenue with all the women standing in the doorways like lines of trap-door spiders (though, Koh did know some of those servers of men, especially, the manager of one establishment, "Blue Rain," who most knew by the name Mina Chae...he knew her as Chae Rei-min...there were several who truly wondered what his relationship/activities were with Chae behind closed doors).

As the two friends continued up, they passed the second off-shooting road nicknamed "Homo Hill" which catered to men and women of a certain taste. Finally, the third street turning up that would lead them to the top.

This way took them past the strangely only mosque in all of that mass seething city and, perhaps, of its location, was also, the site of an important book discovery of sorts by renowned Iranian erotic artist Koonude. While doing some restoration work on the mosque's subterranean basement, more like vault, he discovered a mouldy but intact copy of the "Al Azif."

Just down from the mosque was Abby's. This place is run/owned by Kim Eun-hee and she had turned it into Korea's largest and best used bookstore. It had a spatial feel of what a book selling venue should have with a depth in used books, places to plant oneself and enjoy some of Kim's special coffee and teas, plus, meet others who loved the touch, smell, even tastes of volumes of whatever. It was a cold late winter night, the night of the book signing party, that outer atmosphere didn't stop the Du Voor faithful nor did it effect the store's inner sanctum that had scented burning candles everywhere enhanced with the displayed outré pen and watercolour work of Canadian Tahl Ghitter.

The book event was particularly important to Anne as that night she really wanted to one-up-manship Dr. Koh with her latest find. Koh's only known collectables were his copy of the rare, limited edition of the Lizard King's book of verse "An American Prayer," as well as, equally rare signed hardback release of the poet-King's famed work "The Lords and the New Creatures." Pleased also Koh was to have a copy of the thought insane poet/artist Joseph Gordon's work "A Familiar in a Strange Land." But, this was Du Voor's night, she slipped up nice and tight to her friend and whispered, "I just found for my own the French flagrante delicto 'Le Livre d'Eibon.'" Koh would remember that night.

What jolted Dr. Koh wasn't the pain for he "had learned-like an addict who learns to love the sting of the needle"-to simply absorb what it was: a moment ingrained so primordial, too deeply imbedded to be understood. No, it was the scrape...no, the just skinning, flaying of the Tico's skin that brought him back to the land of reality now. Awaiting...he had long been accustomed to Anne's, for her, fairly recently acquired accessorized perfume...that thing out there just needed one more passing and it would have intercourse with the Tico and hisself.

"Ah Anne, sweet Anne, you would enjoy the irony...cannibalism, what is that, Korean's eat dogs, dog as you know is god spelled backwards and you so loved eating dogmeat in Korea, others, like our friend James, love the wafer and wine...it was survival, and I remembered, remembered a recipe from the section of the Book of Cracked Jade, called "Ritual of the Black Lotus," a book you so craved to read much less own, it suited you so well and filled a real need in James and I. Yes, Anne, you were delicto, delightfully delectable and oh so devoured."

Even James enjoyed the meals, somewhat, we used everything Anne and, one time, upon hearing exactly what it was he was eating, vomited onto the Tico's floor. Yet, even then, he had to do it...you two and your constant puns and word play...James paid homage to you Anne for as he cleaned up the mess, he smiled, "Guess that just goes to show it's true." "Ok, James, you and your Americanisms, I'll bite, what does it prove?" "You just can't keep a good man or woman down."

Now, Dr. Koh lost in this vastness of space, "blinded" not even to see his beloved stars or home, or was it so? He watched, waited...waited...waited no more, as the thing came so easily into.... "I want a good seat at the concert, so move it will you? I hear 'Strange Daze' is one of the best DOORS copy bands around."

"Alright, just let me finish combing my...huh, what on earth?...it's a bloody insect!"

"Hmmm, let's see...it seems almost impaled. Looks like a very tiny, shiny metallic scarab."

"I don't care, off it goes into the toilet"...flush.

The mention of things Korean are true, some of the "speculated answers" for some are purely the fictional imagination of the author.

[Originally inspired by "The Garden of Adompha"]

ARTWORK

Kumiho - Frederick J. Mayer

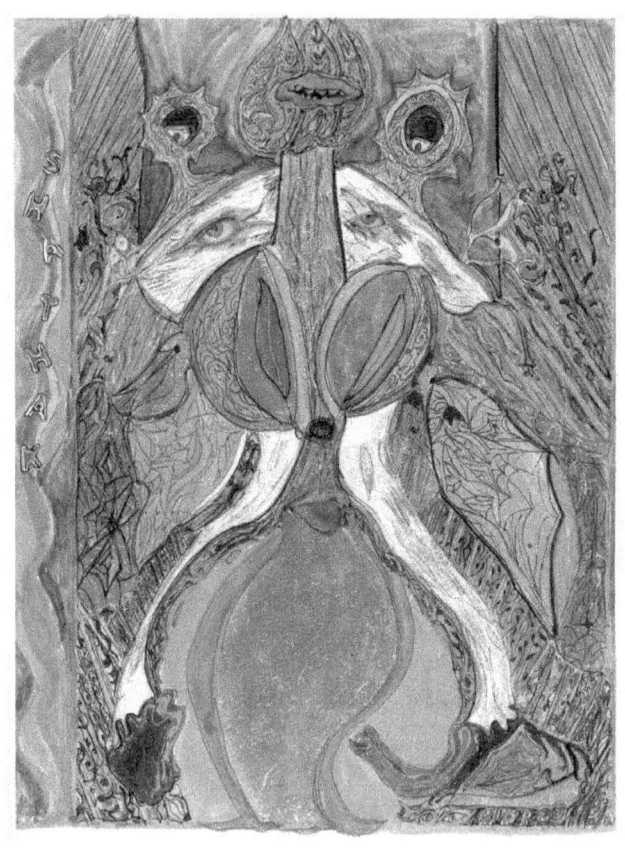

Shathak - Frederick J. Mayer

Tcho Tcho Grand Queen - Frederick J. Mayer

Shathak Masque - Frederick J. Mayer

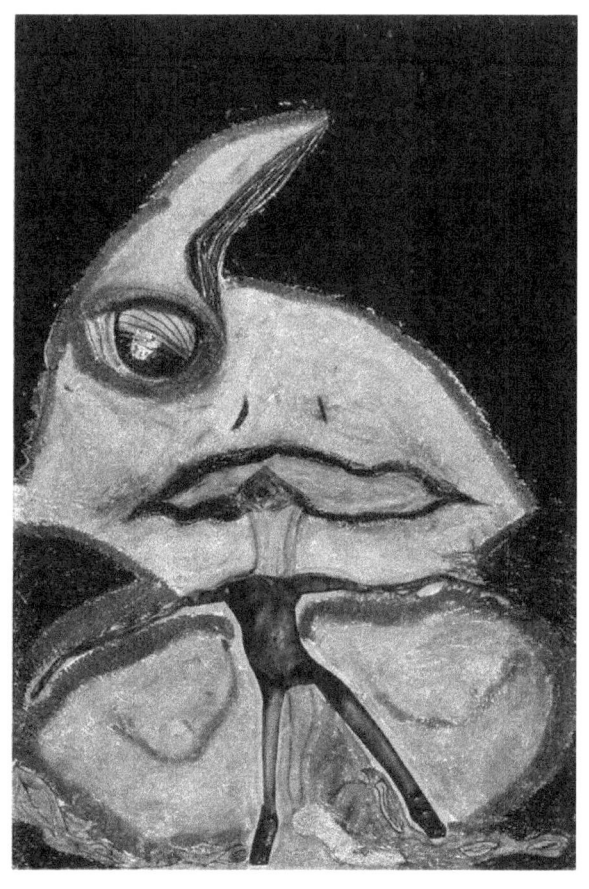

Tsathoggua Mood - Frederick J. Mayer

Our Lady of Lamias Morthylla - Frederick J. Mayer

Flower-woman – Steve Lines

Maal-Dweb - Steve Lines

Malygris - Steve Lines

Ghoul - Steve Lines

NON-FICTION

THE POETRY OF CLARK ASHTON SMITH
By Frank Belknap Long

In a preface to *Odes and Sonnets*, the very beautiful edition of CAS' early poems published by the Book Club of San Francisco circa 1920 George Sterling wrote: "Compared to Smith, Chatterton was a babbling babe." In the eight letters I received from Sterling in the two years preceding his tragic death by his own hand he praised Clark's poetry in even higher terms.

Chatterton was not, of course, a major poet. But when Wordsworth spoke of him as "that marvellous boy who perished in his pride," we can be sure that there were lines in the Chatterton fragments which made Wordsworth feel that if he had gone on and fulfilled his youthful promise he might well have become one of the shining ones—comparable to Burns and Coleridge and Wordsworth himself, who never maintained the slightest doubt as to his own worth.

CAS did not perish in his pride but went on and wrote some magnificent things, both in poetry and prose for the next forty years. But somehow I've always felt that in his early poems he achieved a kind of greatness which he never surpassed, and that Sterling's Chatterton comparison was as critically perceptive as anything that has ever been written about CAS

CAS wasn't a major poet. But he was so glorious a minor one that I believe he will have a place in American letters only just a little below that of Poe, Whitman, Emily Dickinson, Hart Crane, Eliot, Pound, Frost, and e. e. cummings and Robinson Jeffers perhaps. And that is according him very high praise indeed. It's the equivalent of saying that, if he had been a British or Irish poet, he would have been with the best of the minor Elizabethans, or with Francis Thompson or Matthew Arnold (if we exclude Arnold's one major poem, "Dover Beach") or Synge but not, of course, with Shelley or Keats or Yeats.

He has written at least five hundred lines—in perhaps twenty poems—worthy of a major poet at his best. They are traditional poems and preceded the so-called poetic renaissance of 1912–1915 when a new kind of poetry made the "grand line," an unrestrained romanticism, seem difficult to reconcile with the terrible tearing apart of life and experience on all levels which had taken place in the past half century. He was perhaps the last, close-to-last major poet in the romantic genre, and his actual relationship to his age is of less importance. There are few lines in the whole of English literature that have a more granite-like splendour and solemnity than the closing lines of "Memnon at Midnight"—"Ere the dawn restore to ancient ears, the long withholden thunder of his name, and music stilled to monumental stone."

I was still in college when, at [H. P.] Lovecraft's urging, I first got in touch with CAS. I shudder to think how naïve and immature-sounding my first letter to him would seem to me today, since it was one of those fan letters in which all critical judgement is swept aside by an excess of totally uncritical admiration. But the way I felt then about CAS at his best remains pretty much the way I feel about his early poems and not a few of his stories today, except that I have come to believe that it is as a poet that he will be remembered best in the years to come. Like HPL, his serious literary reputation, both in America and in Europe, is becoming too firmly established to be ignored.

I corresponded with him quite extensively for five or six years, and his letters often ran to eight or ten handwritten pages. They were filled with angry denunciations of Auburn's provincialism and he discussed both literature and his growing interest in drawing a sculpture on virtually every page. He sent me perhaps a dozen of his early drawings, some in colour and others in black-and-white. I also possess a letter which HPL sent me, in which Smith discusses Freud as early as 1920 or so. He didn't think too highly of psychoanalysis.

I got in touch with Sterling quite independently, and although Sterling mentioned Smith several times, Smith never, to the best of my recollection, discussed Sterling's poetry, for which he had the highest admiration. I sent Sterling a copy of my *Man from Genoa* and he wrote in reply, "You should do tremendous things in the years ahead." Then he sent me an inscribed copy of *Strange Waters*, and placed *The Man from Genoa* and two other poems in *The Overland Monthly*. He had an "in" there at the time.

The inscription on *Strange Waters* reads, "This shows the stimulating effects of a seaboard climate and frequent visits to the tower of Robinson Jeffers!"

The past, the past!—as HPL would say.

I stopped corresponding with CAS just before Sterling died. I don't know why—it has always been a source of deep regret. But I was corresponding voluminously with HPL, Alfred Galpin, Sam Loveman etc. and sometimes a correspondence will lapse under pressure for no particular reason and is never resumed again.

Nyctalops 7 (August 1972), p. 76.

ABHOTH THE UNCLEAN
By Robert M. Price

In "The Seven Geases" (1934) Clark Ashton Smith borrows from his earlier tale "Ubbo-Sathla" (1933) the notion of a primordial entity, amorphous and protoplasmic, from which all life forms emerged. In "Ubbo-Sathla," a man undertakes a visionary journey (not unlike that of Halpin Chalmers, the doomed protagonist of Frank Belknap Long's "The Hounds of Tindalos") into the remote past and witnesses the great blob of primeval ooze busily and obliviously producing what Smith elsewhere calls "the efts [i.e., salamanders] of the prime." Ubbo-Sathla would then appear to be a kind of microcosmic counterpart to Lovecraft's Azathoth, a cosmic entity resident not so much in space as far beyond it at some dimensional nexus. As Azathoth, a blind idiot Demiurge (as in Gnosticism, from which I have always suspected the concept has been borrowed), creates universe after universe, each with an idiosyncratic set of natural laws, so on tiny earth, Ubbo-Sathla is the unknowing origin point for the production of earth's various life-forms. (And if Azathoth does stem from Gnosticism, my suspicion is that Smith took the name Ubbo-Sathla from an equally esoteric source, Buddhism, where we encounter the term *uposatha* as the name for a meditation ritual.)

Smith, then, has fashioned his own version of the

Lovecraftian genesis whereby mankind was created as a mistake or a joke by the Antarctican Old Ones. For Smith, our origin and destiny are equally meaningless, but for a different reason: we are merely chance products of a disgusting mitosis at the beginning of time. Come to think of it, what Smith seems to have done here is to caricature the process of biological evolution, complete with the nihilistic implications that have always frightened fundamentalist religious believers into a panicked retreat into a new Dark Age. Evolution, too, posits a chance emergence of all creatures, ultimately, from a primordial ooze of amino acids and nutrient slime.

August Derleth, in his passages from the *Necronomicon*, refers to Ubbo-Sathla as "the unforgotten source." Though Steve Behrends has confirmed that this was indeed the original reading of Derleth's manuscript, I feel sure that what Derleth meant to say was "un*be*gotten source." All things were born of Ubbo-Sathla, but Ubbo-Sathla was neither begotten nor born. It is traditional theological language. God is "*autogenes*," self-begotten, i.e., unbegotten. And as the Epistle to the Colossians says all things were brought into being through Christ and will again be "summed up," gathered up, in Christ, so in the end all creatures will somehow return to the undifferentiated mass that is Ubbo-Sathla. The water, so to speak, having managed to rise higher than its unthinking source to become intelligent, will one day sink back to "sea-level." Again, one might compare the long process to that of Continental Drift. As once there existed a single super-continent that we dub "Pangaea" ("the whole earth") or Gondwana (named for a place in India), the tectonic plates upon which the great land masses slowly ride will crash back together, albeit ass-backwards.

I get the impression that Smith intends that in our present time there is no Ubbo-Sathla. There will be again, but remember Smith's protagonist must journey into the past to glimpse the Elder Records clasped in Ubbo-Sathla's embrace. If Ubbo-Sathla had a separate existence in the present, Paul Tregardis could simply have gone to its location to find the tablets.

It looks as if the slime pit of generation visited by Ralibar Vooz in Mount Voormithadreth and called "Abhoth the Unclean" might be the bubbling residue of Ubbo-Sathla, but if so, Smith would seem to have contradicted the conception of Ubbo-Sathla given in that story. But it is obviously supposed to be some version of the same idea, and that might suggest an explanation for Abhoth's epithet "the Unclean." It echoes the very name "Abhoth," which seems meant to suggest "abomination," something hateful. But that is a pun, not the actual meaning of the name. Smith may or may not have known that "Abhoth" means "fathers" in Hebrew, and this name is quite appropriate for the progenitor of all life. But why would a puddle of the primordial ooze, the womb of all terrestrial life, merit the epithet "unclean"? Of course, the epithet is justified in the story by making Abhoth the emitter of loathsome freak-forms, not ordinary creatures of nature. But I think it goes deeper and refers back to the basic Ubbo-Sathla concept of which it is an obvious variant. In what follows, I do not mean to suggest Smith was directly inspired by the sources I will discuss, but I do believe the same conceptual connection was in his mind, a natural and spontaneous parallel.

I believe that Smith had in mind the same basic idea on display in Arthur Machen's "The Great God Pan."

113

There we learn that Helen Vaughan, the precursor to Lovecraft's Wilbur Whateley, was crushing the hope out of her paramours by revealing (apparently in her own devolving metamorphoses, as we see in her death-throes) the undifferentiated state of prime matter from which, a la Plotinus (with whom Machen must certainly have been familiar), is shared by all beings. Earlier, Aristotle had spoken of prime matter as the material "cause" of all things, but it was, as for Plotinus, a logical, not a chronological priority. There had never been a time when such a soup of matter existed by itself (unlike the ancient cosmogonies of India and the Near East, where the cosmos was at first "without form and void," filled with latent potential subsequently activated by some outer force stirring it up like a centrifuge. But Plotinus, unlike Aristotle, assigned a moral value to it. Insofar as it was theoretically unformed, undifferentiated prior (logically prior) to the organization of it into specific forms, it was to be considered *evil*. Plotinus ridiculed Gnostics for branding matter as evil, but his own view was not much different. Matter *had* been (or would be) evil prior to its organization into an ordered world (which is what "cosmos" means). Why?

I believe he had in mind something like the taxonomy of the Bible, where, again, the primal stuff is "without form and void," *tohu* and *bohu*. These common nouns represent a rationalizing demythologisation of an earlier myth of creation by combat, ubiquitous in the ancient world and the prototype of all dragon slayer myths. *Tohu* ('formless, amorphous") is the singular of which the plural is *Tiamat*, the chaos dragon of Sumerian and Babylonian mythology whom Marduk had to defeat in order to create the cosmos and win his kingship over

114

the pantheon. *Bohu* ("void, empty") is the singular form of *Behemoth*, the primal dinosaur-like beast of Job chapter 40, tamed by Yahweh at the dawn of time. This is the background of the Genesis chapter one creation account of the six days plus the Sabbath. It is a specimen of "natural philosophy," pre-technological, observational scientific speculation. It was very much like the speculations of the contemporary Ionian philosophers of Greek Asia Minor. They felt sure that our world of diverse things and forms had begun in a mass of one primordial element. Thales nominated water as the universal substance. Anaximenes thought it was air. Anaximander spoke of it more abstractly as "the Indeterminate Boundless." From the original substance the paired elements had gradually separated out, just as in Genesis: light and darkness, seas versus dry land, the various animal species, etc.

The same biblical writer outlines the traditional taxonomy of his culture in the Book of Leviticus. There the species are differentiated into "clean and unclean." "Clean" animals were those which conformed to the neat categories of creation, and these might be consumed without blame. For instance, fish and cattle were on the menu. But shell fish and pork were not. Why? Because of the stipulated criteria for each category. Fish live in the water and possess fins and scales. The flounder, trout, bass, tuna, etc., qualify. Shellfish live in the water, but they lack fins and scales. Cattle are defined as having cloven hoofs and chewing the cud. Beef is kosher because cows have cloven hoofs and chew the cud, but pigs are not kosher because, though their hoofs are cloven, they have but a single stomach and do not ruminate the same mouthful of cellulose again and again.

These poor creatures who fall between the stools, who are neither fish nor foul, are "unclean." They are "abominations," *tebhel*, literally "mixings" or "confusions." They have a bit of *tohu* and *bohu* in them, a whiff of the primordial chaos that God shaped into an ordered cosmos—mostly! The loose ends were off limits. And since their chimera-like character was itself a derivation from the pre-philosophical, mythical *Tiamat* and *Behemoth*, foes of the creator, they were evil. Thus that which partakes of the pre-cosmic chaos is unclean and abominable.

So is Abhoth, and for the same reasons. The defective creatures it spawns down there in the caverns consist of single, animated limbs, rolling heads, etc., and these are reflections of the "defective" character of the non-kosher beasts of Leviticus, hence unclean.

Deeper still, the twin tales of Abhoth and Ubbo-Sathla reflect the primordial anxiety of the human race over whether human beings are the product of two parents like themselves, or the spawn of the earth. This concern, so strange-sounding to us, probably stems from very early times when primitive people began to make the connection between sex and procreation, a major concern of the Garden of Eden myth in Genesis chapters 2-3, where Adam ("red earth"), formed directly from the ground, is warned never to eat of the Tree of the Knowledge of Good and Evil, which turns out to hold the secret of *carnal* knowledge as the means of procreation. Sampling this fruit along with Eve, whom God had created essentially as a sister to Adam, the earth-born man turns his back on his earthly origin and turns to sexual procreation. Terrible consequences ensue.

As Claude Levi-Strauss interprets the Oedipus myth

116

cycle, it concerns the same dilemma. The deep structure of the familiar story depicts the early human discovery of sex as the cause of birth as well as, I think, the anxiety of children, led to believe they were, e.g., discovered under a cabbage leaf, when at puberty they learn about sex. It is a sea-change in thinking that will lead to a whole new world of anxiety. The lesson of all such myths is that the transition to sexual knowledge and the embrace of one's human origins at the expense of a belief in direct descent from Mother Earth is necessary but painful. We feel forever after that we are being punished for denying the idyllic earth-origin.

The horrific revelation of Ubbo-Sathla and Abhoth, with the attendant dangers (Tregardis is reabsorbed and loses his identity) is symbolic of the alienation between human-born humans and the earth, whom they have betrayed by departing from "trading her underfoot." Ubbo-Sathla/Abhoth is the primal elemental stew equivalent to the clay of Eden, the womb of Gaia. And we no longer get along. That's why these stories of Smith's are horror stories, tales of alienation from the cosmos. And, as I hope to have demonstrated, they are also genuine myths.

A SEVENTIES SORCERER ON THE SMALL SCREEN
By Brian M. Sammons

Clark Ashton Smith was a poet, sculptor, painter, and author of fantasy, horror and sci-fi stories. He was a member in very good standing of the Lovecraft Circle who created some of the Big 'Uns of what's commonly referred to as the Cthulhu Mythos. He dreamt up the sorcerer Eibon, the book penned by that wizard that shares his name, and even the Great Old One Tsathoggua. That last one Lovecraft loved so much that he name-dropped that terrible toad-like deity in a number of his own weird tales. Continuing to compare Smith to Lovecraft, Clark wrote more stories than Lovecraft, lived far longer, and was equally well regarded by his peers and the critics. Yet while H.P. Lovecraft has only increased in popularity as the years moved on, Smith has been forgotten by all but his most faithful fans. Nowhere is this more evident than in the world of cinema. There have been dozens of films based on stories by HPL, and even more that have been heavily influenced by him. Then there's the small screen, where Lovecraftian themes and creations popped up in anthology shows like Night Gallery, Masters of Horror, and even cartoons such as The Real Ghostbusters, South Park, and Scooby Doo.

And yet no love for Klarkash-Ton on any screen,

big or small.

Well, almost.

In 1972 the network television horror anthology, Night Gallery, created by Twilight Zone mastermind Rod Serling, had as their first episode of what was to be their last season an adaptation of a Clark Ashton Smith story. This would be the first and sadly only time any of Smith's stories would be captured on film. (1)

The episode in question was based on Smith's "The Return of the Sorcerer", a tale of dark magic set in the modern day. The original story is a relatively short, straightforward bit of horror, and I wish that so too was the Night Gallery episode. At just twenty-five minutes in length, it is short, but it has been stuffed by a whole bunch of extras Smith had never intended. Worse, not a one of the additions enhanced the story in any way.

The basics of the Smith tale remains, with a translator of Arabic going to work for strange man as a research assistant and secretary. Right off the bat, the mini-movie gets some cool points for casting Bill "The Incredible Hulk" Bixby as the unwitting assistant, who undergoes a name change from the story for some unknown reason, going from Mr. Ogden to Noel Evans. Everyone's favourite ghoulish actor, Vincent Price, plays the creepy demonologist named Carnby with a book that needs translating and a dark secret to hide. In addition to the name change, a new character has been shoehorned into the TV plot in the form of a cute blonde named Fern. She acts as a general servant, and perhaps concubine, for Price's weirdo, and an obvious love interest for Bixby's character. And by obvious, I mean that within ten minutes of the two meeting each other, they're already making out.

Mr. Ogden, oops, sorry, I meant 'Noel' is tempted into taking the job by the big bucks offered. Too bad he must also live in Carnby's spooky mansion. How spooky is it, you ask? Well there are literally drifting fog banks in the hallways. Yeah, that's pretty damn spooky, although no one really seems all that put off by the fog. Must be a 70's thing. Oh and as if that wasn't enough of a clue for Noel to GET OUT a la The Amityville Horror, there are other subtle clues to be found. Like later at dinner it's Noel, kooky Carnby, flirtatious Fern, and a real live black goat that sits in a chair and eats at the table with everyone else. Yes, a black goat, who Carnby introduces as his father, "who is now back with us" and goes by the name, The Fallen Tower. Uh-huh.

And that right there is the biggest problem with this interpretation of Smith's story. It makes far too unnecessary changes. It also mixes in mystical mumbo jumbo from various sources such as numerology, black goats, the names of Old Testament devils, upside crosses, and little bon mots like, "Did you know, that for every sorcerer there are a thousand sorceresses?" All these additions not only felt like unnecessary padding, but often like bad comedy, such as the goat at dinner, or when Fern makes out with a frog. No, really.

The things that are in both the Smith story and the Night Gallery episode are the constant mentions of something scurrying in the halls, that Carnby insists are rats, and that eventually the assistant translates the Big Book O' Evil ™. He tells Carnby that the tome says a sorcerer can come back to life after death, even if chopped up into little bitty pieces. As soon as he says that, everyone watching the show knows what's going to happen next. Especially once Noel learns that Carnby murdered and hacked up his twin brother, who was a powerful sorcerer, just a few days back.

Yes, I'm sorry to say that neither the Smith original story nor this short film was very surprising. However, while the story had some great creepy buildup to the inevitable horrifying conclusion, the TV show once again veers wildly off in another, and far less effective, direction. I won't ruin the surprise of the story, although I'd really be surprised if you couldn't guess it, because I think you need to read it. However I am not so charitable when it comes to the Night Gallery episode, so consider the following paragraph a SPOILER ZONE and skip over it if you want to.

After a few rubbery-looking hands and feet crawl around the house's halls, the evil dead twin puts himself together, menaces the twin that killed him (Vincent Price supplying twice the ham in a dual role) with a sword, chants mystical and quasi-satanic gibberish for a bit and then…I don't know. Turns the other brother into another black goat? The TV show is never clear as to what happens, and has an odd and unsatisfying ending with Bixby's translator continuing to live in the old house with Fern, his lover and possible familiar. Yep, that's the best way the writers of the teleplay thought to end the story.

In and of its self, the Night Gallery episode isn't horrible. It keeps the basics of Smith's story, has Bill Bixby doing his calm, sedate thing he would later perfect on The Incredible Hulk and Vincent Price doing the insane and spooky act he had mastered years before. It is (unintentionally?) funny at times with the goats, frogs, fog, seventiestastic dialog, and other silly bits. However as the one and only adaptation of a Clark Ashton Smith story to film, it is rather disappointing. Seek it out for

121

some grins and giggles, if nothing else, but Klarkash-Ton deserves better.

There is talk of a very independent film done in 1975 on super 8 film that practically no one has seen outside of the filmmakers based on Smith's "The Double Shadow".

CLARK ASHTON SMITH IN CARMEL
Scott Connors

Early in 1911, Clark Ashton Smith began a correspondence with George Sterling, the uncrowned king of northern California's Bohemians, which would last until the elder poet's death. Sterling was then living on his own property just outside the village of Carmel-by-the-Sea. He had settled there in 1905, along with the novelist Mary Austin and photographer Arnold Genthe, partly because of the low cost of real estate, and partly because the developers were seeking "residents who would form a lively, cultured community" and encouraged "writers, artists, musicians, and university professors to buy in the area" (Walker 9). The aftermath of the 1906 earthquake further hastened this exodus from San Francisco. Carmel was home to a thriving colony of creative types by the time Smith and Sterling came into contact. Some of this even rubbed off on the ordinary people of the village: the *Los Angeles Times* half-jokingly reported on May 22, 1910 that "The plumber of Carmel has subscribed to the Harvard Classics; the butcher reads Browning, and the liveryman wears long hair" (Walker 92). Some of the prominent writers and artists who came to Carmel included Jack London, Jimmy Hopper, Upton Sinclair, William Rose Benét, Xavier Martinez, Ambrose Bierce, and Sinclair Lewis.

Sterling first invited Smith to visit him at Carmel in a letter dated May 19, 1911, barely five months after they began to correspond. Sterling was tremendously impressed by Smith's poetic prowess, all the more so because of his youth (Clark was barely eighteen when he received his first letter from Sterling), and wished to mentor him in the same fashion that he had himself been mentored by Bierce. Smith reluctantly declined the invitation, citing his father's ill health, while expressing a hope that a visit would be possible the next summer. Sterling repeated the invitation early in October, and urged CAS to come down sometime before Christmas, emphasizing "that the only expense you'll be put to is the fare" (*SU* 30). Smith's response:

> How I wish I were down in Carmel with you! I am not at all certain whether I can get away this winter or not. If I do come, it probably won't be before December. I am so tied down that the way is not at all obvious now. I'd rather be able to accept your invitation than have the "Abyss Ode" accepted—even by the "high and mighty" North American Review! Auburn is nothing but a cage, and with little gilding on the bars at that. (*SU* 31)

Little did Sterling suspect just how impoverished were Smith's circumstances. This changed when Robert Haven Schauffler, a friend of Sterling and fellow protégé of Ambrose Bierce, visited Smith in May 1912; his letter to Sterling apparently does not survive, but it undoubtedly reported the impoverished conditions in which Smith and his parents were living. Sterling expressed gratitude that Schauffler had made the visit, "as his words seem to draw you nearer to me and make you less of a mythical being" he wrote to Smith (*SU* 48). Sterling repeated his invitation that Smith pay him an extended visit in Carmel, not only offering to pay Smith's expenses both ways but also to provide his impecunious colleague with "a partially-worn outing-suit … with golf-stockings and tennis-shoes." (*SU* 48)

Smith had almost met Sterling the previous November, when he visited San Francisco for a couple of days as guest of Boutwell Dunlap, an attorney and former consul to Argentina who had met Smith in Auburn. Sterling was staying at the Bohemian Club in San Francisco at the time, and each day Clark tried to reach him by telephone, but without success. Years later Smith confided to his wife Carolyn that Sterling was otherwise engaged with a girl friend at an apartment he kept on Montgomery Street for such assignations, and thus "too busy" to meet with anyone else.

The afternoon of June 28, 1912 was mild and overcast when Sterling took a horse and wagon and drove to the train station in Monterey to meet young Clark. Much to his surprise, Smith was not on the train. The conductor had mistakenly told Clark to get off at San Jose, and as a result he had to purchase another ticket to Monterey. Smith walked the remaining four miles to Carmel, arriving at approximately nine o'clock. Years later he recalled that "There were no other people on the road and it was very beautiful" (Wakefield) as he walked in

> the thickening dusk through a country that was thrillingly new and strange to me. Some dweller on the outskirts of Carmel steered me vaguely in the general direction of Sterling's house. The road ran obscurely through a black forest starred with infrequent lights, and seemed to end at the last visible light. A woman … redirected me. I had only to cross a wooden footbridge and follow a narrow, winding path down the ravine. There, in the pine-fragrant darkness, I came to the blurred outlines of a cabin and a house; I knocked on the cabin's door. A high, cracked, New England voice sang out, "Come in, Clark Ashton Smith!" (*PD* 59–60)

Sterling's wife, Carrie, was not living with him at the time, and Smith apparently never met her. Sterling's house was occupied at the time by John Kenneth Turner and his family. Turner was a journalist whose muckraking book *Barbarous Mexico* had exposed the frightening social inequalities existing under the Diaz dictatorship; it has been credited by some as the spark that ignited the Mexican Revolution. His wife, Ethel Duffy Turner, was the daughter of a guard at San Quentin Prison; her brother later became a reform-minded warden at the same institution and an early opponent of capital punishment. She would later edit a literary journal called *The Wanderer* that would publish several of Smith's poems. Sterling had been occupying the cabin he had built for Nora May French, the beautiful and tragic poetess whose suicide by cyanide in 1907 was the first in a series of self-inflicted deaths among the Carmelites that would not end until Sterling's own death in November 1926. Sterling let Smith have the cabin, while he himself moved into a tent on the village side of his property. Smith would later recall how

> George told me to keep the cabin door shut at night. "If you don't," he warned, "the cat will come in and jump on the bed. You'll think it's Miss X____ trying to climb into bed with you, and you'll be scared." "Oh, no," I rejoined, "I'll probably think it's Nora May's ghost, and I won't be scared at all. I'm sure that her ghost would be a lovely one." "You certainly have an imagination," he commented, half admiringly, half deprecatingly. (*PD* 61–62)

"Miss X____" was Alma Duffy, Ethel Turner's "pretty teenage sister," to whom Clark "was attracted in a shy sort of way" (Turner). Alma recalled years later how Sterling confided to her the hope that she would provide Clark with a "romantic interest and poetry would flow," ruefully adding "I wasn't … it didn't." Clark did not make a favourable impression upon the Turners. In a memoir that she prepared for the Bancroft Library, Ethel wrote:

> While we were still living in his house, a young poet, Clark Ashton Smith of Auburn, California, came at George's invitation to visit him. Clark lived on a farm and had very little schooling. He educated himself by reading the dictionary. He read George's poems, probably in *The Testimony of the Sons* and *A Wine of Wizardry* and became his worshipper, writing poems in the same style, that he sent to George. George liked the poems and was flattered by the obvious imitation of style. So he invited Clark to visit him. The boy came, shabby and unkempt, and George quickly got him into knickers and jacket.

Alma wrote to her sister that "I remember he would go to town with me to pick up groceries. We had to walk along a path through the woods. I'd end up way ahead of him. When I glanced back, there he would be ambling along in a daze." Later she would ask a boy she knew who lived in Auburn if he knew Clark and received this response: "Alma, don't tell me you know that nut. He had his head in the clouds and all the kids thought he was weird."

Henry Dumont wrote in *A Faun on Olympus*, his unpublished biography of Sterling, that Clark "was of a lonely, dreamy disposition, not easily making acquaintances, and generally preferring his own society to that of other people. The dominant note in his poems was a rapt remoteness from earthly things."

Ethel recalled how Sterling was "rather in a quandary about entertaining Clark," but Clark apparently never noticed. "Almost every morning," he would write in "George Sterling: Poet and Friend," "George took me on a round of calls, often distributing surplus game

127

among his friends." There were frequent trips to the shore in search of the elusive abalone, since immortalized in "The Abalone Song," a communal chant begun by Sterling but added to by others, including Clark. At night they would gather on the beach with the day's catch, or else prepare complex "mulligan stews," which Sterling would cook up in a big black pot (Ingels).

One particularly notable day that was well remembered by all who participated was July 5. On that day Sterling rented a "tally ho" (a type of pleasure coach) and four horses from the village stables, and took Clark and the Turner family to Soberanes Point for a picnic. Clark recalled a multitude of sea fowl that might have seemed familiar to King Euvoran, while Alma Duffy remembered that "there were rocks to climb about, in the water. We saw sea anemones, sea urchins and star fish."

Sterling took Clark to see two plays at the Forest Theatre, an open-air amphitheatre, the oldest west of the Rockies, established in 1910 by Sterling's friend Herbert Heron, which is still in operation today. A reporter for the *San Francisco Chronicle* wrote of the "sense of mystery of the theatre itself, with the fog floating along the pine tops and the sound of the surf forming a pulsing background to the play" (Walker 79). Sterling took Clark to see Bertha Newberry's play "The Toad" on July 3. This is somewhat surprising, since Sterling and Heron had ridiculed the play as "preposterous" and "full of plagiarisms," most of which were derived from Heron's play "Montezuma." On July 5 Clark saw "Alice in Wonderland" performed. These were probably the first plays that Clark had ever seen.

This idyllic month came to an end on July 25, 1912. George and Clark travelled to San Francisco, where Clark had several photographs taken by Bianca Conti (1874?–1954), a prominent portrait photographer of that period, one of which was laid in as a frontispiece in some copies of Smith's *The Star-Treader and Other Poems* (1912). After staying overnight at the home of Sterling's friend Roosevelt Johnson, Clark returned to Auburn and George went back to Monterey. While they would meet several more times over the years, the halcyon days of July 1912 would never be repeated. Carrie Sterling, no longer able to tolerate her husband's infidelities, left him late in 1914. George would end up living in New York City for a couple of years, and while he would eventually return to California, he would never return to his home in Carmel.

WORKS CITED

Dumont, Henry. *A Faun on Olympus.* Unpublished manuscript, Library of Congress.

Ingels, Beth. "Fun With Food: A Poet Concocts Mulligan, Chioppino." *Monterey Peninsula Herald* (5 May 1960): 23.

Schultz, David E. and S. T. Joshi, ed. *The Shadow of the Unattained: The Letters of George Sterling and Clark Ashton Smith.* New York: Hippocampus Press, 2005. (*SU*)

Smith, Clark Ashton. "George Sterling—An Appreciation." In *Planets and Dimensions: Collected Essays of Clark Ashton Smith.* Ed. Charles K. Wolfe. Baltimore: Mirage Press, 1973. (*PD*)

———. "George Sterling: Poet and Friend." In *Planets and Dimensions.* Ed. Charles K. Wolfe. Baltimore: Mirage Press, 1973.

Sterling, George. Carmel Diaries. Unpublished manuscript, Bancroft Library (BANC MSS C-H 60).

Turner, Ethel Duffy. *Notes on George Sterling and on Carmel's literary colony, 1966.* Unpublished manuscript, Bancroft Library (BANC MSS C-H 174).

Wakefield, Carolyn Smith. *The Man Who Walks the Stars.* Unpublished manuscript, John Hay Library, Brown University.

Walker, Franklin. *The Seacoast of Bohemia.* Rev. ed. Santa Barbara, CA: Peregrine Smith, Inc., 1973.

Appendix:
The Abalone Song

By George Sterling, Clark Ashton Smith, and others

Oh, some folks boast of quail and toast,
Because they think it's tony;
But I'm content to owe my rent
And live on Abalone.

Oh, Mission Point's a friendly joint
Where every crab's a crony;
And true and kind you'll ever find
The clinging Abalone.

He wanders free beside the sea
Where 'er the coast is stony;
He flaps his wings and madly sings,
The plaintive Abalone.

On Carmel Bay, the people say
We feed the Lazzaroni
On Boston Beans and fresh sardines
And toothsome Abalone.

Some live on hope, some live on dope,
And some on alimony;
But my Tom Cat and I get fat
On tender Abalone.

Oh, some drink rain, and some champagne,
Or brandy by the pony;
But I will try a little rye
With a dash of Abalone.

Oh, some like jam, and some like ham,
And some like macaroni;
But bring to me a pail of gin
And a tub of Abalone.

Some stick to biz, some flirt with Liz,
Down on the sands at Coney,
But we, by Hell! Stay in Carmel,
And nail the abalone.

We sit around and gaily pound,
And hold no acrimony,
Because our object is a gob
Of toothsome abalone.

Our servant girl is sure a pearl—
Her name is Meg Mahoney:
You ought to see the way that she
Serves up the abalone

He hides in caves beneath the waves—
His ancient patrimony;
And so 'tis shown that faith alone
Reveals the Abalone.

The more we take, the more they make
In deep sea matrimony;
Race suicide cannot abide
The fertile Abalone.

Oh, some throw rice, and some throw dice,
And some throw cascaroni,
But Eve, by hell, will throw a spell
Around the Abalone.

I telegraph my better half
By Morse or by Marconi;
But if the need for speed arise,
I'll send an Abalone.

Oh, some folks think the Lord is fat,
Some think that He is bony;
But as for me, I think that he
Is like an Abalone.

Oh! Some are named for persons famed,
And some are named Mahoney
But when I get a kid, you bet
I'll name it Abalone.

A MACHEN REVIEW OF CLARK ASHTON SMITH

Scott Connors

The first few decades of the Twentieth Century could well be called the Golden Age of the Weird Tale, since writers on both sides of the Atlantic were writing a new type of supernatural horror story that was rooted in the modern psyche as opposed to mere variations on traditional Gothic themes. In Great Britain writers such as Arthur Machen, Algernon Blackwood, M. R. James, Lord Dunsany, H. Russell Wakefield, William Hope Hodgson, and others were producing the work for which they would become best known, while a few years later American writers associated with H. P. Lovecraft, including Henry S. Whitehead, Donald Wandrei, and Clark Ashton Smith, would begin to produce material every bit the equal of their British cousins, albeit differing somewhat in style, approach, and subject matter. There was little if any contact between the two sides of the Atlantic during Lovecraft's lifetime: Donald Wandrei had exchanged a few letters to Arthur Machen, and Machen was acquainted with Vincent Starrett, a sporadic correspondent of Lovecraft, as well as Harold Wolf, a Cleveland, Ohio newspaperman who wrote the first newspaper article on Lovecraft. M. R. James had expressed disgust with the American type of tale and dismissed Lovecraft's essay *Supernatural Horror in Literature*. The discovery, then, that Arthur Machen had reviewed a poetry collection by Clark Ashton Smith, who would later become perhaps the only contemporary American writer to rival Lovecraft for the ability to evoke a sense of cosmic dread, is of more than a little interest.

After attempting to earn a living on the stage for the first decade of the last century, in 1910 Arthur Machen accepted a position as a chief reporter with *The Evening News*. He had been selling articles to various magazines for some time, "and it seemed only a step at the time from selling articles to magazines." Machen later referred to this period as the "prostitution of the soul," because as Wesley Sweetser observed "for the first time in many years he had to work at the direction of an outside force rather than in conformance with certain subjective standards."(16) Mark Valentine describes Machen's duties thus: "He was at first used for all-around reporting duties of a trivial kind which he found intolerable—interviewing the famous he found embarrassing—but was gradually allowed to become an acknowledged feature writer on favourite subjects such as traditions and ceremonies, the byways of London, and religious matters, as well as doing book reviews." (97)

This later was one of the least objectionable of Machen's duties. An examination of Sweetser and Goldstein's bibliography shows that roughly a third of his known contributions to *The Evening News* were book reviews of one sort or another, although, with few exceptions, the titles under consideration were not listed. Many of these titles found their way to Machen's desk in the traditional form of review copies sent by the publisher, but sometime early in 1916 a colleague of Machen's gave him a copy of *The Star-Treader and Other Poems* (San Francisco, California: A. M. Robertson, 1912) by Clark Ashton Smith (1893-1961), then a youth living in the foothills of the Sierras, who was a protégé of George Sterling, the "uncrowned king of Bohemia" and the unofficial Poet Laureate of California. Smith's poetic debut was greeted by the West Coast press with some enthusiasm: they called him "the Boy Keats of the Sierras" and ranked his work with Shelley and Byron. *The Star-Treader*, his first collection of poetry, received favourable reviews from both the West Coast papers plus such organs of the eastern establishment as *The New York Times*, the *Boston Evening Transcript*, and *Current Opinion*, although his extensive vocabulary and cosmic themes met with some bewilderment.

The manner in which the book came to his attention is of itself of some interest. Smith's father, Timeus, was an expatriate Englishman who had travelled the world before settling in Auburn, California, a small town in the heart of the gold mining country near Sacramento, where he married a woman a few years his senior and started a family late in life. He maintained contact with his relatives in England through correspondence, and some of these letters still survive in the Clark Ashton Smith Papers at the John Hay Library of Brown University. One such relative, a nephew who signed his name only "Willie," wrote in a letter dated February 13, 1916 the following:

Well now I have some good news for Clark Ashton. At least I hope it will be so. Let me tell you the story fully.

In the "Mail" we get some lines by a man who signs himself "Touchstone," and even when we were up in Lancashire my friend & me [*sic*] used to wonder who he was, as his work was very good.

A few weeks ago he published a volume of his "war-poems," & in giving publicity to the book the "Mail" printed his photograph.

As soon as I saw this I felt I had seen the face somewhere. I set to work following the clues which told me that a man I had seen in the train was "Touchstone." I was determined to speak to him if my surmise was the correct one. A fortnight ago my opportunity came as he was alone in the same carriage with me. Needless to say my deductions were right & when I suggested that he might be the one he was quite taken aback & wondered how I had found out.

Now my idea was to give to him the books by Clark for a criticism & you will be glad to know that he not only promised to receive a copy, but also that he would put it before the reviewer of the paper. I took up the "Evening News" on Saturday & was agreeably surprised to find a review of the book by no other than Arthur Machen. He is the author of the "Bowmen" & the phantasy of the "Angels of Mons." I should think he is our greatest writer to-day & what he says is very important.

I enclose his review. I hope I was quite right in saying Clarke [*sic*] was 17 when he wrote most of the work! Anyway the review is on the whole very good & coincides with my humble opinion.

"Touchstone" was the pseudonym of Claude Edward Coleman Hamilton Burton (1869###1955), who had published a volume of poetry called *Fife and Drum*, as by "Touchstone" of "The Daily Mail" and "C.E.B." of "The Evening News." in 1915. Burton apparently felt that Smith's book was more in Machen's line than his own, and so passed the volume along. It would have been simple for Machen to ignore the book entirely, but instead he wrote the following review (which, incidentally, is not listed in Sweetser and Goldstone), which appeared in *The Evening News* for Saturday, February 12, 1916, under the heading of "Books of Today:"

Seventeen often longs to write, above all to write poetry; and seventeen usually makes a sad mess of it, and spends long years of anxiety afterwards, lest some enemy discover that thin volume of sorry verse.

It is understood that Mr. Smith is seventeen; but he at least will never blush for "The Star-Treader." He is not far from the true vision of the world.

Fairy Lanterns
'Tis said these blossom-lanterns light
The elves upon their midnight way;
That fairy toil and elfin play
Receive their beams of magic white.
I marvel not if it be true;
I know this flower has lighted me
Nearer to Beauty's mystery.
And part the veils of secrets new.

The author shows in many of his verses a great admiration for "the grand manner;" he builds his poems up as if they were cathedrals.

Often he is justified by his results; but one would urge him to admire above all simplicity and lucidity. Rheims Cathedral is###or was, alas!###a miracle of rich adornments; but how lucid, how clear and self-illuminating is the vast scheme of the west-front.

My colleague Don Herron points out that Machen's opening statement, that Smith would never have to be ashamed of verses he scribbled at the age of seventeen, is of no small significance when we remember that Machen's first book, *Eleusinia* (1881), was written around that age, and that Machen later tracked down all but two copies of this title and destroyed them. In the context of Machen's life, then, this was high praise indeed. The selection of "Fairy Lanterns" for quotation is interesting in light of Machen's own tales of the Little People ("The Novel of the Black Seal," "The Shining Pyramid," etc.), and also for the lines "I know this flower has lighted me/Nearer to Beauty's mystery,/And part the veils of secrets new," since viewing the realities beneath the surface of life was a major theme in Machen's work, from "The Great God Pan" onward. Much of the rest of the volume deals with astronomical and/or mythological themes, and is endued throughout with what H. P. Lovecraft would later describe as a sense of "Cosmicism," which he defined as the "capacity to feel profoundly regarding the cosmos and the disturbing and fascinating quality of the extra-terrestrial and perpetually unknown." (Lovecraft, *SL*III.196). Lovecraft identified Machen as one of the supreme Cosmic masters, writing in his monograph *Supernatural Horror in Literature* that "Of living creators of cosmic fear raised to its most artistic pitch, few if any can hope to equal the versatile Arthur Machen . . . ." (421) Smith derived his Cosmicism from his mentor, George Sterling, the author of such poems as "The Testimony of the Sun" and "A Wine of Wizardry," who combined the aesthetic teachings of his Master, Ambrose Bierce, with the scientific materialism of Ernst Haeckel to create a new aesthetic in reaction to Victorian didacticism which displaced man as the central facet of creation. Machen, however, did not share this particular worldview, being essentially a mystically-inclined Anglo-Catholic with a desire to penetrate the mysteries of the sacraments whereby man might achieve reunion with the Godhead, something which Lovecraft later recognized. Smith's own version of Cosmicism differed greatly from Lovecraft's, since like Machen he rejected materialism and embraced a worldview that was almost neo-platonic. At the same time Smith, like Lovecraft, rejected a homocentric viewpoint in preference of an "imaginative escape from the human aquarium." (*SL* 145) In many ways Smith's aesthetic represents the midpoint between those of Lovecraft, the materialist, and Machen, the mystic.

Arthur Machen was one of Clark Ashton Smith's favourite writers. In a letter to George Sterling dated August 28, 1919, CAS wrote "Thanks for 'The Hill of Dreams,' the reading of which has given me considerable pleasure. Much of it is very beautiful and subtle. Am I to keep the book?" I have another of Machen's books, entitled: 'Hieroglyphics,' one of the best things on literature and literary values that I have seen for a long time, apart from the writings of John Cowper Powys," which indicates that he had read Machen before Lovecraft. (*SU* 174) Later in his life CAS listed Machen's "The Novel of the White Powder" among his favourite weird stories. (*PD* 41) It is somewhat surprising that Smith never mentioned that Machen had ever seen any of his work. Smith never mentioned this review in his correspondence with Sterling, Lovecraft, R. H. Barlow, Donald Wandrei, August Derleth, Samuel Loveman, or any of the other writers with whom he corresponded, whose letters from Smith are still extant. In later years Smith would list with defiant pride the various prominent writers and persons who had praised his work: David

Starr Jordan, the first president of Stanford University; Ambrose Bierce; Edwin Markham; Alice Meynall; Vachel Lindsay; Benjamin De Casseres; and, of course, Sterling. Arthur Machen is conspicuous by his absence. The clear inference is that Smith felt that the review was not, cousin Willie to the contrary, "on the whole very good."

One possible reason for this may be found in the reference to his age when he wrote the poems. In general tone Machen's review is not dissimilar to one by the poet Stephen Phillips from *The Poetry Review* which, while also praising Smith's poetic promise, also dwelt upon his lack of years. Smith showed a distinct lack of appreciation of Phillips' review. (*SU* 85) Machen praises Smith when he says that CAS will never have to be ashamed of these early verses, but in correspondence Smith appears particularly sensitive to characterization of his work as being by "the human equivalent of a five-legged kangaroo." (*SU* 60) Sterling himself warned a correspondent that "the child has a sense of humour, but not about himself." (Gross 12). Machen's urging of Smith "to admire above all simplicity and lucidity" is surprising in light of Machen's own style, which is certainly closer to that of Smith than, say, that of Theodore Dreiser or Ernest Hemingway, but this may also have disappointed Smith. What is important about this review is Machen's acknowledgment that not only is Smith's poetry atypical for his age, but that "He is not from the true vision of the world," as seen by Machen. That Machen recognized this common thematic ground is the true significance of this review, and while we might wish that he had seen fit to devote more column space to a discussion of Smith's Cosmicism, or a comparison of Smith's great dramatic monologue "Nero" with those of Browning and Tennyson, it is clear that when we list the honour roll of those who recognized Smith's art the name of Arthur Machen will occupy a prominent place.

Thanks are due to Peter Cannon, for his help in locating a file of *The Evening News* and for making the photocopy; to Mark Brown of the John Hay Library, for his assistance with the Clark Ashton Smith Papers; and to S. T. Joshi, for his assistance in identifying possible candidates for the review, and for providing [with David E. Schultz] copies of the Smith-Sterling correspondence from the New York Public Library.

WORKS CITED
Gross, Dalton, ed. "George Sterling's Life at Carmel: Sterling's Letters to Witter Bynner." *Markham Review* 4 (1973), 12-16.
Lovecraft, H. P. *Selected Letters III*. Ed. August Derleth and Donald Wandrei. Sauk City, WI: Arkham House, 1971. (*SL*III)
—. *Supernatural Horror in Literature*. In Dagon *and Other Macabre Tales*. Ed. S. T. Joshi. Sauk City, Wisc.: Arkham House, 1987.
Machen, Arthur. "Books of Today." *The Evening News*, London (12 February 1916): 4.
Phillips, Stephen. "Voices from Overseas" (review of *The Star-Reader* [sic] *and Other Poems,* by Clark Ashton-Smith [*sic*]), *The Poetry Review*, 2 (1913): 141.
Smith, Clark Ashton. *Planets and Dimensions: Collected Essays of Clark Ashton Smith*. Ed. Charles K. Wolfe. Baltimore, MD: Mirage Press, 1973. (*PD*)
—. *Selected Letters of Clark Ashton Smith*. Ed. David E. Schultz and Scott Connors. Sauk City, WI: Arkham House, 2003. (*SL*)
— and George Sterling. *The Shadow of the Unattained: The Letters of George Sterling and Clark Ashton Smith*. NY: Hippocampus Press, 2005. (*SU*)
Sweetser, Wesley D. *Arthur Machen.* New York: Twayne, 1964.
Valentine, Mark. *Arthur Machen.* Mid Glamorgan, Wales: Seren, 1995.
"Willie." Letter to Timeus Smith, February 13, 1916, manuscript,

Clark Ashton Smith Papers, Brown University.

The Emperor of Dreams
Donald A Wandrei
With an introduction by Scott Connors

In 1912 there came from the press of A. M. Robertson, in San Francisco, a slender book of poems. Had that volume come from a well-known writer, it would have, ranked him with the immortals. Had it come from a rising author, it would have spread his fame far and wide. It came from neither. It was little advertised, for it had no financial backing and the author had neither influential friends nor acquaintances among those who determine what the public may read. No attempt was made to popularize it. The book shortly passed from sight, almost unknown save to a few fortunate people who possessed copies. The book was, *The Star-Treader and Other Poems*; its author, Clark Ashton Smith, a young poet, not yet twenty, who had already dreamed and dared to dream as few men have in a lifetime. That book of poems is one of the great contributions to American literature. It contains some of our finest pure poetry, some of our best imaginative lyrics. A few of them would now be famous, had they been written by a Keats or Shelley, and a cause of laurels. The critics have ignored the volume. The literary pontiffs have passed it over. Today, not many persons know it, even by title. Yet the same critics decry the anæmic state of American letters, its lack of enduring works. A genius—in the true, not abused, sense—appears, his eyes on the other side of eternity, his poems of eternity, his work the kind that endures. He is unnoticed. He is given no encouragement. American poetry is still anæmic.

A thousand years hence, when the people of that distant time survey the accumulated mass of all literature, they will place high up on the roll of honour the name, Clark Ashton Smith; and looking backward, they will ask why the world of that age long ago did not appreciate him when it had him. Perhaps -this is as it ought to be. The man of letters should be the possession of those who do appreciate him. It is not given to ordinary man to walk with the gods; nor, when it is so given, does he usually avail himself of the opportunity unless he is one of that group which is the justification of himself, the cornerstone of the arts, and the prophet of. immortality.

A poet can not live on visions, on dreams, on a prospect of future fame. He must live on something more material. And one can not write when it is necessary to earn a sustenance. Perhaps this was the reason that ten years elapsed before another book appeared under the poet's name. Or perhaps it was the neglect, popular, which is of little importance, and critical, which may be of the greatest importance, given his first book. Or perhaps the dreamer lived in his own realm, indifferent to ephemeral external life, writing seldom and then mainly for his own pleasure. Or perhaps . . . One trembles at the thought. "Ebony and Crystal" was published in 1922. Its fate is akin to that of "The Star-Treader." Not many persons know it. Those who do regard it as worshippers a sanctum sanctorum, as connoisseurs a rare tapestry, as jewellers a priceless pearl. (I have since been informed that the silence was due to the destruction of imperfect poems, and to ill-health. It is hard to believe this statement in a day when the least is treasured by those whose best is mediocre. But it explains the uniform excellence of his work, the lack of a single weak poem.)

There is no place in contemporary prose and poetry for genius.

Was "Ebony and Crystal" worth the labour of ten years? It is a larger volume than the first and contains twice as many poems, one hundred and fourteen against fifty-five. Did eleven poems a year, and those not of unusual length, with one exception, justify the author a place among the front-rank poets? If fame is the criterion, no. If excellence, yes. "Ebony and Crystal" is the finest volume of pure poetry that has appeared in America since the opening of the twentieth century, perhaps the finest since the time of Edgar Allan Poe. Not until its publication did any of our poets approach him in imaginative power. "Ebony and Crystal" belongs on that shelf with Poe, Coleridge, Blake, Shelley, Baudelaire. In that group where each is coequally supreme, he may justly take his place.

Imagination is his god, beauty his ideal; his poems are an offering to both. He is the poet of the infinite, the envoy of eternity, the amanuensis of beauty. For even as beauty was deity to Keats and Shelley, so it is to him. and in its praise has he written. But he has not celebrated it as an abstract term or an aesthetic quality, but as a more tangible substance. He has constructed entire worlds of his own and filled them with creations of his own fancy. And his beauty has thus crossed the boundary between that which is mortal and that which is immortal, and has become the beauty of strange stars and distant lands, of jewels and cypresses and moons, of flaming suns and comets, of marble palaces, of fabled realms and wonders, of gods, and daemons, and sorcery. Time and Space have been his servants, the universe his domain; with the stars his steeds and the heavens his tramping ground, he has wandered in realms afar; and he has found there a wondrous beauty and a strange fear, the goal of his early dreams and the enchanted road to greater, all manner of things illusory and fantastical.

Some of his poems are like shadowed gold; some are like flame- encircled ebony; some are crystal-clear and pure; others are as unearthly starshine. One is coldly wrought in marble; another is curiously carved in jade; there are a few glittering diamonds; and there are many rubies and emeralds aflame, glowing with a secret fire. Here and there may be found a poppy- flower, an orchid from the hot-bed of Hell, the whisper of an eldritch wind, a breath from the burning sands of regions infernal. The wizard calls, and at his imperious summons come genie, witch, and daemon to open the portal to the haunted realms of faery; and their wonder is transmuted so that those who can open the door may listen to the murmuring waters of Acheron, or watch the passing of a phantom throng; and the fen-fires gleam; and the slow mists arise; and heavy perfumes, and poisons, and dank odours fill the air. A marble palace rises in the dusk, a treasure-house of gold, and ebony, and ivory; soft lutes play within; fair women, passionless and passionate, wander in the corridors; silks and tapes- tries adorn the walls, and fuming censers burn a rare incense. And fabulous demogorgon and hippogriff guard the golden gateway to the hoarded wealth. The sky is black. But now and again white comets blaze, or suns of green, or crimson, of purple, flame across the firmament with silver moons.

The sky is burning. Stars hurtle to destruction or waste away. All mysteries are uncurtained. One may watch a landscape of the moon, the seas of Saturn, the sunken fanes of old Atlantis, wars and wonders on some distant star.

There is no place in the poetry of Clark Ashton Smith for the conventional, the trite, the outworn. It is useless to search his work for offerings to popular desire. Some authors pander to the public taste; their books may have a huge sale, but die with the author. Some writers have skill and ability but desire wealth or immediate fame; their work has not so great a popularity but endures longer. A very few have what is called "genius." They write primarily for themselves, or with a certain small group of people who know literature in mind. They are artists, word artists; and they fashion their prose or poetry with care and labour. They are seldom appreciated in their lifetime, and never have widespread popularity, but the highest minds of every age enjoy their work. These are ones who speak to us across the ages, who will speak across the ages to come. It is to this class that Clark Ashton Smith belongs. One will examine his poems in vain for the commonplaces that have so largely crept into our literature; and by so much as he has avoided ephemeral and written of immortal things, by so much the longer will his work endure.

II

"The Star-Treader" was his earliest volume, and it shows the effects of imagination in its first exuberance. Stars and suns and comets parade in all their majesty; Chaos. Infinity, and "the eldritch dark" are ever present; and the wonder, the inexplicable mystery of the Universe form the background of the book. It was then that the young poet wrote "The Song of a Comet;" it was then that he fashioned "The Song of the Stars;" and from his pen came "The Wind and the Moon." Of the fixed forms, the sonnet was his favourite, and nearly a third of the poems have its form. In most of them he strove to obtain single, dominant effects, to limn one unforgettable scene, as in "The Last Night," "The Medusa of the Skies," and "Averted Malefice." Occasionally, he was content with a single quatrain, or a pair, as "The Maze of Sleep" and "The Morning Pool." But-he had a greater chance to display his power in the longer, more sustained poems, such as "Saturn," "The Star-Treader," and "The Masque of Forsaken Gods." They would have been accomplishments for a man of maturity, for one who had long written poetry, as the work of a youth they are remarkable achievements. The entire book has this note of maturity; it was a world-weary youth wise beyond his years who wrote these poems beautiful, fantastic, sometimes bitter and more than once inexpressibly terrible in their suggestion. "The Star-Treader" was published in 1912. Not for ten years did another book come from the poet. ("Odes and Sonnets" was privately issued by the Book Club of California in 1918. The odes are from "The Star-Treader"; the sonnets were included in "Ebony and Crystal.") What had he been doing those ten long years? Had the neglect of his first book compelled him to turn his mind into other channels? It is hard to say, but "Ebony and Crystal" is not a large volume for the work of ten years.

There is a great difference between the two, in imagery, in tone and subject, and in metrical skill. The first was, to some extent, experimental; the second, a fulfilment of the promise in the foreshadowing work. The craftsmanship of these later poems is well-nigh flawless; the volume is rich in perfectly planned, perfectly fashioned jewels. It is jewel-cutting that he was engaged in those ten years. Here may be found "such stuff as dreams are made of," and the dreams themselves; here the utterance of god and witch, the harmony of the spheres, the strains of immortal music, the unveiling of an imagery unparalleled. The beauty of these poems is intoxicating, for the poet who wrote them was haunted and intoxicated by loveliness immaculate and incarnate, by all beauty. And the poems are couched, not in ordinary language, but in an English filled with curious and archaic forms, rare or obsolete words, unusual diction; and they have been given flowing rhythms and unforgettable melodies; and they move in measured intonation, and in cadence, and in musical sweep that are seldom found in poetry. They are whispers of the unearthly, rather than mortal work. They are enduring forms of unenduring dreams and ideals and desires. They are the unattainable, set in deathless words of gold. They are time-outlasting marble; they are lotus and poppy; they are fadeless amaranth and asphodel, pure, perfect shadows of the pure and perfect, eternal, aeonian. They are star-dust and starshine, caught by a dreamer of the ages, fashioned in ebony and crystal. They are nectar and ambrosia, nepenthe, Lethean draughts to drown the world in forgetfulness and oblivion. They are the waters of paradise.

The poems are laden with a pagan, exotic beauty and imagery. Some- times this takes the form of light and shadow, as in "Arabesque." Sometimes it deals with the lands of romance, as in "Beyond the Great Wall:"

> Beyond the far Cathayan wall,
> A thousand leagues athwart the sky,
> The scarlet stars and mornings die,
> The gilded moons and sunsets fall.
> Across the sulfur-coloured sands
> With bales of silk and camels fare,
> Harnessed with vermil and with vair,
> Into the blue and burning lands.
> And, ah, the song the drivers sing,
> To while the desert leagues away-
> A song they sang in old Cathay,
> Ere youth had left the eldest king.
> Ere love and beauty both grew old,
> And wonder and romance were flown.
> On fiery wings to worlds unknown,
> To stars of undiscovered gold.
> And I there alien words would know,
> And follow past the lonely wall,
> Where gilded moons and sunsets fall,.
> As in a song of long ago.

Occasionally it reverts upon itself as in "The Melancholy Pool" and "Solution:"

> The ghostly fire that walks the fen,
> Tonight thine only light shall be;
> On lethal ways thy soul shall pass.
> And prove the stealthy, coiled morass.
> With mocking mists for company.
> On roads thou goest not again.
> To shores where thou hast never gone,-

Fare onward, though the shuddering queach
And serpent-rippled waters reach
Like seepage pools of Acheron,
Beside thee; and the twisten reeds,
Close raddled as a witch's net,
Enuind thy knees, and cling and clutch
Like wreathing adders; though the touch
Of the blind air be dank and wet,
As from a wounded Thing that bleeds
In cloud and darkness overhead-
Fare onward, where thy dreams of yore
In splendour drape the fetid shore
And pestilential waters dead.
And though the toad's irrision rise,
As grinding of Satanic racks,
And spectral willows, gaunc and grey,
Gibber along thy shrouded way,
Where vipers lie with livid backs,
And watch thee with their sulphurous eyes,-
Fare onward, till thy feet shall slip
Deep in the sudden pool ordained,
And all the noisome draught be drained,
That turns to Lethe on the lip.

But usually it takes the form of a rich imagery,
oriental in its profusion and splendour, unlimited in its
concept and scope, imperishable by reason of its
supreme, its unearthly, its ' alien perfection. "In Saturn"-

Upon the seas of Saturn I have sailed
To isles of high, primeval aramant,
Where the flame-tongued sonorous flow'rs
enchant

The hanging surf to silence: All engrailed
With ruby-corode pearls, the golden shore
Allured me; but as one whom spells restrain,
For blind horizons of the sombre main,
And harbours never known, by singing prore
I set forthrightly: Formed of fire and brass,
Immenser skies divided, deep on deep
Before me,-till, above the darkling foam,
With dome on cloudless adamantine dome,
Black peaks no peering seraph deems to pass,
Rose up from realms ineffable as Sleep!

"The Kingdom of Shadows," "The Land of Evil Stars," "A Precept," "Chant of Autumn," Requiescat in Pace,"-but it is useless to try to select fine poems from a volume which has room for none other.

There is one long poem, however, that deserves special attention. It is "The Hashish-Eater," containing many hundred lines of blank verse. But it is far different from what is usually called blank verse, from what, one knows as ordinary iambic pentameter. This has always been a stately metre, capable of impressive effects; and in his hands, with the aid of his boundless imagination and descriptive powers, besides his technical skill, it has become the implement of a. poem- colossus, gigantic in theme and treatment, told in a heavy, sonorous English that sweeps onward in measured roll with an ever-swelling rhythm from the Imperial summons of the opening lines:

Bow down: I am the emperor of dreams:
I crown me with the million-collared sun
Of secret worlds incredible, and take

152

Their trailing skies for vestment, when I soar,
Throned on the mounting zenith, and illume
The spaceward-flown horizons infinite.

And at the very end of a volume which will one day
be a prized literary heritage is the sombre and morbidly
magnificent prose-poem, "The Shadows," a poem told
with such care that no word is lost or wasted, and so well
that it lingers in the memory as a sable fantasy enshrined,
a rare perfume, darkly odorous and darkly poisonous,
clinging to a bit of strangely shapen ebony.

III

In October, 1925, cane the third of his published books,
"Sandalwood," a volume which, though slender, contains
more poems than his first. After "Ebony and Crystal," not
much could be added to his laurels, but had that volume
not exist- ed, "Sandalwood" might have taken its place to
a large extent. It is different from "Ebony and Crystal" in
that the poems are less ambitious with regard to the
depicting of strange, vast splendour, but more songlike,
lyrical, and spontaneous, though the mastery of technique
and the metrical skill displayed admit of neither
spontaneity nor its attendant roughnesses. The poems
may be divided into several classes, including nineteen
translations from Baudelaire, and four songs from the
uncompleted romantic drama, "The Fugitives," And there
is a poem of six stanzas, "We Shall Meet," told in an
original or very rare but very beautiful verse form. But to
one who has read the early work of Clark Ashton Smith,
his later poems remain beyond praise. One may go into
ecstasies at a vision of glory; but the greater glory

surpasses description. And he who has sate on the ramparts of Heaven and Hell is mute before magnificence and pageantry that shame the speech.

No critic and no criticism can do justice to the work of this poet. There are some things which are beyond the reach of both, and in this rare group belongs the work of Clark Ashton Smith. For there are books so distinctive, so excel- lent, that they can not be compared with others of their class, by reason of their perfection. For them, there is no standard of judgment, and one can only admire what one is helpless to censure or to sanctify. To use homely language in estimating such work is to do it an injustice; and yet. superlatives are equally useless, for they have been so carelessly employed that nowadays they deprecate the work they are meant to extol.

Earlier in this essay, certain other poets of the romantic-imaginative group were mentioned. But Clark Ashton Smith can not be associated with any particular one. Each within that class was original, and by virtue of a similar originality, this modern poet deserves his rank. The great poets neither follow nor imitate; they create. And he has created, on a cosmic scale. The greatest indictment of contemporary verse is its lack of form, its deliberate exclusion of the most vital quality of a work of art, a quality which every book that aspires to greatness must have, above all else, if it is to endure. Substance-form; form-substance; of the two, form is by far the most important. And this element-including, as it does, diction, style, presentation, euphony, craftsmanship-is present in the poems of Clark Ashton Smith to such an extraordinary degree that, had there been no substance, had he produced only rainbows and iridescent bubbles, he would still have deserved lasting attention. Indeed, the sole flaw in his poems is occasionally form in too great a degree. His gifts are so much beyond those of average poets, and his vocabulary is of such enormous content that the desired word is often an uncommon one. Yet even this lends a curious charm, a singularly effective atmosphere to the poem, at worst, it may only be considered what would be a god-send to the lamentably word-base verse of the Philistines. It is an example of his innate power of concentration, his ability to say best and to say beautifully the things that deserve to be clothed in costly raiment.

Just where the place of this emperor of dreams will ultimately be fixed in poetry can not, of course be foretold, save that it should be very high. Nor can one prophesy the day he shall receive the recognition he has earned. It took the world forty years to appreciate Thomas Lovell Beddoes; it took longer for it to appreciate William Blake; Arthur O'Shaughnessy is still almost unknown; and few even of those occasional persons who have read "The Book of Jade" could tell the name of its author, Park Barnitz. And now, Clark Ashton Smith-

ADDENDA TO
CLARK ASHTON SMITH: LETTERS
TO H. P. LOVECRAFT

In July 1987 Necronomicon Press published Smith's letters to Lovecraft, as edited and annotated by Steve Behrends. Mr. Behrends utilised the letters deposited by R. H. Barlow as part of the Lovecraft Papers at the John Hay Library. During my own researches in the late 1970's, I was fortunate to uncover some additional letters and postcards. Printed here for the first time are a series of postcards which Annie Gamwell returned to Smith as a *momento mori* after Lovecraft's death. Smith in turn gave these cards to Helen Sully, from whom I obtained copies when I visited her at her home in Auburn.

The numbering system is adapted from that of the Necronomicon Press edition. Since the first letter occurs before any of those in that book, I have assigned it the number [-1]. On all other items, I have assigned a number corresponding to the entry in the Necronomicon Press edition closest to the item chronologically, with letters appended in order.

Those who complain about the occasional lack of legibility in Lovecraft's letters should try transcribing Smith's postcards; they will never complain again afterwards! I was assisted greatly in deciphering Smith's holograph and in annotations by David E. Schults and S. T. Joshi. In editing these texts Smith's sometimes inconsistent practices concerning story and book titles have been made consistent, so short stories are referred to in quotation marks, while book and magazine titles are italicized. Where Smith underlined a word, we have italicized it; however, where he double-underlined a word, we have followed his usage.

I am grateful to William A. Dorman, representative of the Estate of Clark Ashton Smith, for permission to print these letters.

[25a] *Postcard from Clark Ashton Smith to H. P. Lovecraft, post marked January 2, 1932:*

Dear E'ch-Pi-El:

This will give you an idea of the country near Auburn.

I have your letter and will write before long.

Wright has just accepted *Avoosl Wuthoqquan.*[1]

Yrs in the lore of the infra-red runes,

Klarkash-Ton

[27a] *Postcard from Clark Ashton Smith to H. P. Lovecraft, postmarked May 14, 1932:*

Dear E'ch-Pi-El:

---

[1] "The Weird of Avoosl Wuthoqquan," *Weird Tales*, June 1932.

This will give you an idea of the local canyon scenery.

Your letter to W. must have done some good he has accepted *Ubbo-Sathla*,[2] which I sent him again not long ago!

Yrs, in the name of the cromlech geelos,

Klarkash-Ton

[30a] *Postcard from Clark Ashton Smith to H. P. Lovecraft, postmarked May 24, 1932:*

Dear E'ch-Pi-El:

Have just read *The Dreams in the Witch House*, which is *grand* stuff and magnificently written. Ugh! One isn't likely to forget Brown Jenkin in a hurry. Here is some more of our savage wilderness. You'd get a kick out of these terrific gorges. Yrs, Klarkash-Ton

[32a] *Postcard from Clark Ashton Smith to H. P. Lovecraft, postmarked August 10, 1933:*

Dear E'ch-Pi-El:

---

[2] "Ubbo-Sathla," *Weird Tales*, July 1933.

This view of Auburn may interest you. Averaud's mansion³ is indicated aming trees just below vertical arrow in middle background. The slope at extreme upper right is the beginning of the hill on which I live. House of the fair priestess of Hyperborea⁴ is in portion of town (not shown) on extreme left. Yrs/, under the seal of Thasaidon,

Klarkash-Ton

[*On front*: Mansion of the Evil Devotee/ Old Winery/ Hill about the Shrine of Tsathoggua.]

[32b] *Postcard from Clark Ashton Smith to H. P. Lovecraft, postmarked August 17, 1933:*

Dear E'ch-Pi-El:

You should have been here on Monday last the mercury notched itself at 109¹, and the wind was like the breath of a forest fire.

Hornig⁵ writes me that Gernsback has just made him managing editor of *Wonder Stories*!!**!!!

Klarkash-Ton

---

³   The setting for The Devotee of Evil first published in *The Double Shadow and Other Fantasies* (Auburn, Ca.: Auburn Journal Press, 1933), rpt. in *Stirring Science Stories,* February 1941.

⁴   Helen Sully, who visited Lovecraft in the summer of 1933.

⁵   Charles D. Hornig, editor/publisher of *The Fantasy Fan.*

[32c] *Postcard from Clark Ashton Smith to H. P. Lovecraft, postmarked August 21, 1933:*

Dear E'ch-Pi-El: Yr letter received, and will write soon. This is another view of Auburn, looking east from the grounds of the County courthouse the domed building in first view that I sent.

The seventh adjuration of Yig seems to taken [*sic*] effect against the serpent people.

Yrs/, Klarkash-Ton

[32d] *Postcard from Clark Ashton Smith to H. P. Lovecraft, postmarked August 28, 1933:*

Dear E'ch-Pi-El:

I shall write soon. I am doing the IX Chapter of Eibon at present a start on that much-requested cycle of occult elder lore! Have also written *The Witchcraft of Ulua* and *The Tomb Spawn*, tales of Zothique. The End joineth the Beginning! Yrs ever, Klarkash-Ton

[32e] *Postcard from Clark Ashton Smith to H. P. Lovecraft, postmarked August 29, 1933:*

Dear E'ch-Pi-El: Thanks for card. Hornig writes me that Gernsback really is in a hole and is anxious to pay authors. Well, I hope the last item is true. Our weather has gone autumnal; a grey sky of smoke and fog, with mercury falling to 541 or 561 at sunrise, and the sun burning dimly at noon.

Will write at length in a day or so.

Yrs, Klarkash-Ton

[33a] *Postcard from Clark Ashton Smith to H. P. Lovecraft, postmarked September 14, 1933:*

Dear E'ch-Pi-El: Thanks for views of Quebec, and congratulations on your trip! It must have been magnificent. . . Chap. IX of Eibon not yet released. Of course, I have had to suppress the more frightful portions and unbearable implications and have deleted many hideous details anent *The Coming of the White Worm.* Have written a four p. note on M. R. James for TFF.[6] One William Crawford of Everett, Pa., writes saying that he plans to start a mag of weird and sc. fiction called *Unusual Stories* no pay. Yrs under the Yellow Sign,

Klarkash-

Ton

[33b] *Postcard from Clark Ashton Smith to H. P. Lovecraft, postmarked September 16, 1933:*

---

6 "The Weird Works of M. R. James," *The Fantasy Fan*, February 1934.

Dear E'ch-Pi-El: Letter and views received.   Many thanks! Will write ere long and return Hall's letters.[7] A. S. sounds promising under this regime, and I hope it will live up to its promise. IX Chapter of Eibon now completely rendered from old French ms. of Gaspard du Nord; who, as you recall, figured in *Ylourgne* . . . But, as Eibon himself says, this history of the White Worm's advent is told with such omissions as are needful for the sparing of mortal weakness and sanity. Even at that the slaying of Rlim Shaikorth and the day long streams of blackness that poured from his cloven bulk, is pretty strong. Yrs, Klarkash-Ton

[33c] *Postcard from Clark Ashton Smith to H. P. Lovecraft, postmarked October 2, 1933:*
Dear E'ch-Pi-El: Thanks for that view of the Peaks of Thok!   Donner was no great climb, but afforded a magnificent prospect!! IX Chapter of Eibon went forward to you some time ago. Wright has not yet returned the ms but give him time. Nothing yet from A.S. they must be digesting the weird material that I sent in at leisure. I look forward to re-reading your monograph with the new additions, and feel highly honoured that you should have mentioned my tales among the standard items. *The Seven Geases*[8] is about finished a hell of an underworld itinerary! Weather here has gone back to mid-summer warmth, reaching the lower nineties yesterday. Of course, I still have my paraphernalia outdoors. Yrs under the seal of sixtystone[9], Klarkash-Ton

---

7   Desmond Hall, associate editor of *Astounding Stories.*
8   *Weird Tales*, October 1934.
9   A reference to Arthur Machen's "The Novel of the Black Seal."

[34a] *Postcard from Clark Ashton Smith to H. P. Lovecraft, postmarked October 5[?], 1933:*

Dear E'ch-Pi-El: That relay of news from Wright on your last card was certainly encouraging. Knopf ought to know a good thing when he sees it.

Astounding has taken *The Demon of the Flower.*[10] It is certainly encouraging if they will buy work so out-of-the-way as that yarn, which Wright and Clayton thought too recherche.

Of course, Wright sent back the Eibon chapter. Says he will use it, however, if times ever improve also the *Vathek* episode.[11]

Weather continues warm, seldom falling below 701 even at night. I am rewriting an old tale, *The Disinternment of Venus,*[12] but will start some new work pretty soon.

The Witchcraft of Ulua will come to you from Barlow. You may find it instructive to see what is barred from W. T. on grounds of censorship.[13] Yrs, Klarkash-Ton

[34b] *Postcard from Clark Ashton Smith to H. P. Lovecraft, postmarked October 10, 1933:*

---

10 *Astounding Stories*, December 1933.

11 "The Third Episode of Vathek," first published in R. H. Barlow's *Leaves*, I (Summer 1937).

12 *Weird Tales*, July 1934.

13 Wright accepted this story after Smith deleted some suggestive passages. The original text was published in *The Unexpurgated Clark Ashton Smith*, and is currently available in *Tales of Zothique* (West Warwick, R. I.: Necronomicon Press, 1995).

Dear E'ch-Pi-El: Your letter and enclosure rec'd. Have called *every* malediction in Le *Livre d' Eibon* on that philistine jackass, Knopf, and am now about to search the Pnakotic Mss. for new curses.**!!** I am glad that my rendering of IXth chapter was not too rotten. Have done a drawing of Tsathoggua which I'll send in my next letter. Maybe it would help Lumley to identify that evil entity! An Indian neighbour recognized the picture as representing what he called one of the *Old Boys*! More anon.

Klarkash-Ton

[35a] *Postcard from Clark Ashton Smith to H. P. Lovecraft, postmarked November 6, [1933?]:*
[Salutation missing]: Weather is still clear and calm, though with fog in the valley below. Mercury fell to 441 last night too chill for outdoor penmanship. Sorry about W.'s returned check it must have been on that rotten Fletcher bank. Mine seems to have gone through all right so far. Yes, the circulars of *Unusual* are good: I'm afraid the s.f. fans will raise a howl about the pure fantasy element. *Astounding* is now banning the weird because of such protests. ***Just had an order for the D.S. from Trinidad, British West Indies also one from Mexico. The *Geography of Witchcraft* [14] came. Yrs for the elemental Azoth,

Klarkash-Ton

[35b] *Postcard from Clark Ashton Smith to H. P. Lovecraft, postmarked November 24, 1933:*

---

[14] By Montague Summers.

Dear E'ch-Pi-El:

Thanks for the *Connoisseur,* which came last night. I'll send you *The Geography of Witchcraft* and *The Lady Who Came to Stay*[15] whenever you want them. *Brood of the Witch Queen*[16] is out at present; but I'll round it up when I have the chance. I was a little vexed by Brother Hornig's scoop in utilising my letter about Eibon, etc.[17] He asked me where and how the books could be obtained; and I didn't think to stipulate that the answer was for his private information! Dumb of me, I'll admit. However, as you say, the hoax might easily go too far. Klarkash-Ton

[35c] *Postcard from Clark Ashton Smith to H. P. Lovecraft, postmarked December 6, 1933:*

[No salutation]

15
  By R. E. Spenser (New York: Knopf, 1931).

16
  By Sax Rohmer.

17
  A reference to Hornigs article "Startling Fact," *The Fantasy Fan,* November 1933, which prints a portion of a letter from CAS to Hornig revealing that such eldritch tomes as the *Necronomicon* and the *Book of Eibon* were in fact invented as story props. Smith's letter is published as On the Forbidden Booksin *Planets and Dimensions,* ed.Charles K. Wolfe (Baltimore, Md.: Mirage Press, 1973), p. 29.

Picture on back shows the uptown section of Auburn as seen from courtyard of local high school. Yr last received. Thanks for impressive view of Providence State House. *Geog. Witchcraft* and *Lady Who Came to Stay* will go forward to you very shortly. Hope you have received *The Seven Geases*. Wright says he wants another look at the ms., so am instructing Ar-Ech-Bei to forward it directly to the Chicago Satrap after his perusal.[18] Weather in this section of the citrus belt is fit for Dante's frozen circle. Yrs in the name of Michael Scott,

Klarkash-Ton

[39a] *Postcard from Clark Ashton Smith to H. P. Lovecraft, postmarked March 7, 1934:*

Dear E'ch-Pi-El:

The book arrived yesterdayBmany thanks! A. Vigalis[19] is full of treasures, and I am enjoying the Wakefield stories. *The Cairn* strikes me as being perhaps the best.

Spring is apparently full-blown in these parts mercury went up to 701 yesterday. Hope there won't be a return to brumal *rigours.*

Hazel Heald's story in the current W.T. is very good.[20]

Yrs.,

Klarkash-Ton

---

[18] *Weird Tales*, October 1934.

[19] Arthur Weigall (1880-1934), author of *Wanderings in Roman Britain* (1926).

[20] "Winged Death," *Weird Tales*, March 1934. Lovecraft had revised this story.

[39b] *Postcard from Clark Ashton Smith to H. P. Lovecraft, postmarked March 23, 1934:*

Dear E'ch-Pi-El:
Thanks for card. Will write soon. Hope you will have rec'd *The Green Round* and *Others Who Returned* ere now. Glad you are enjoying Prorok[21] no hurry at all about returning the book. You are dead right archaeology is a vast and little-tilled field of imaginative possibilities. Hope that Prorok will suggest some stories to you. That card of lower Auburn represents the town all right; but the coach, etc., was placed for the occasion. Weather here is fast turning into summerBno rain, and the grass already beginning to turn yellow. Hope your monsoons are over. Yrs for the brazen tower of Tsathoggua,

Klarkash-Ton

[41a] *Postcard from Clark Ashton Smith to H. P. Lovecraft, postmarked June 15, 1934:*

Dear E'ch-Pi-El: Letters and enclosures rec'd and will answer shortly. Thanks for snapshotsBthese show you very well under a large reading-glass. Am anticipating the recordsBalso *The Shunned House.* Not much news hereBthe weather has gone screwy with fog, cloudiness, thunderstorms, and what not. Wright plans to use one of my drawings of Tsathoggua with *The Seven Geases.* Yrs

Klarkash-Ton

---

[21] Count Byron Khun de Prorok, author of *Digging for Lost African Gods* (1926).

[42a] *Postcard from Clark Ashton Smith to H. P. Lovecraft, postmarked July 23, 1934:*

Dear E'ch-Pi-El: I've been intending to write for weeks and will answer yr letter soon. Recently enjoyed a 2nd visit from the Peacock Sultan.   Little news otherwise, except that Wright has taken *Xeethra*[22] and Gernsback has remitted 50 pazoors on account! Will send on shortly some books by W. Hope Hodgson, which H. Koenig loaned me and said to forward to you. Under the Black Seal, Klarkash-Ton

[42b] *Postcard from Clark Ashton Smith and Donald Wandrei, postmarked November 21, 1934, 5 PM:*

Dear E'ch-Pi-El:
        Melmoth and I are holding a session among my wizard towers!   Wish you were here to utter the third incantation!
                        Klarkash-Ton
        [Wandrei's portion not included.]

[42c] *Postcard from Clark Ashton Smith to H. P. Lovecraft, postmarked April 5, 1935:*

Dear E'ch-Pi-El:

---

[22] *Weird Tales*, December 1934.

Thanks for loan of highly interesting Rio de Janeiro epistle. . . . will write soonBam running a hospital single-handedly at present with both parents laid up. Sold *The Chain of Aforgomon*,[23] *The Treader of the Dust*,[24] *The Black Abbot*,[25] and *Necromancy in Naat*[26] to the capricious satrap of weirddom!!! Out of the Eons is damn good! ugghh! Those eyes!

Klarkash-Ton

[43a] *Postcard from Clark Ashton Smith to H. P. Lovecraft, postmarked September 7, 1935:*

Dear E'ch-Pi-El: This view will give you some idea of the older and more atmospheric part of Auburn.

I'll write soon have been more or less under the weather, with domestic conditions little if at all improved. Have managed to execute a few more eidola, and should have some of the best ones photographed ere long. I'll be glad to hear from Ar-E-ch-Bei, and am hoping that his plan for printing my verses will materialize. Yrs in the faith of the Old Ones, Klarkash-Ton

[43b] *Letter from Clark Ashton Smith to H. P. Lovecraft (on four postcards), typed., undated:*
[written between November 1935 and February 1936]:

---

[23] *Weird Tale*, December 1935.

[24] *Weird Tales*, August 1935.

[25] "The Black Abbot of Puthuum," *Weird Tales*, March 1936.

[26] *Weird Tales*, July 1936.

Meridian of the black plenilune

Dear E'ch-Pi-El:

I had meant to acknowledge your card of condolence before this, but seem to have fallen into a deplorable habit of general procrastination. Letters, even the most necessary ones, seem to remain unwritten.

The blow of my mother's passing has been a heavy one for us[27]; but it is some consolation that she went with little or brief suffering. She was able to walk about and talk within a few minutes of the final stroke. My father has borne up pretty well, all things considered; and I have been compelled to take a little care of myself, and have now gained back some of the weight and energy which I lost during the summer.

Writing has been in abeyance; but I have managed to do a few more carvings. It is surprising what one can do, by ~~with~~ the utilization of odd moments that would otherwise go to waste. I really think that these little sculptures have about saved my life, since they have given me a new interest and preoccupation at a time when I needed it most. Some of the results obtained are so unusual (I have worked out various modes and tricks of treatment, including a hardening process for the finished carvings) that I believe the sculptures would puzzle many

---

[27] Mary Frances (Fanny) Gaylord died on September 9, 1935.

professed experts. I'll have the promised pictures taken soon and will send you copies. Later, I'll loan you a few actual specimens by express, if you'd care to see them. It occurs to me that we might have a little fun with Morton by submitting some of the most ancient and mysterious-looking ones for his appraisal, with an appeal for information as to the problematic art-age and civilization to which they belong! However, it probably wouldn't do to let him think that I have any connection with the carvings!

Two pieces, *Dagon* and *The Outsider*, were inspired by your stories. I think I shall have to be unselfish and make you a gift, presently, of *The Outsider*. Other pieces, done during the past summer and fall, are entitled: *The Goblin, Saber-Toothed Nightmare, Devil-Chick, Atlantean Warrior, Lemurian Ghost, Swamp-Feeder, The Sorcerer Transformed* (a Goya subject), *Asmodeus, the Black Pan, The Great Head, The Gargoyle, Temple Guardian, Young Elemental, Ouroboros, Hyperborean Snake-Eater, Chinese Magistellus; The Blemmye, Maiden Blemmye, The Inquisitor Morghi, The Terminus, Thibetan Demon* (a Janus-faced horror) and *The Death-God of Poseidonis*.

Ar-Ech-Bei sent me *The Shunned House*. He has certainly done a creditable job on the binding! The story itself holds up superbly on re-reading. The disciple of Krang seems determined to put out my Incantations, and I certainly hope that his plan will materialize.

Yours for the eating of the black lotos [*sic*],
Klarkash-Ton

[43b] *Postcard from Clark Ashton Smith to H. P. Lovecraft, February 5, 1936:*

171

Dear E'ch-Pi-El: This is to acknowledge your letter and the loan of the Hersey-Dodd production.[28] Many of the drawings are surprisingly good and compare favorably with those of Alastair[29] and other post-Beardsley artists. Will write before many daysBalso start the carvings on their travels. Yrs.,

Klarkash-Ton

[43c] *Postcard from Clark Ashton Smith to H. P. Lovecraft, postmarked May 22, 1936:*

Dear E'ch-Pi-El:

I've just read *The Shadow out of Time* with prodigious pleasure, and must congratulate you on a magnificent piece of work. Will write soon at length. Trust the carvings will reach you presently and will not prove a disappointment. Yrs, in the faith of Nyarlathotep,

Klarkash-Ton

[43d] *Postcard from Clark Ashton Smith to H. P. Lovecraft, postmarked October 13, 1936:*

Dear E'ch-Pi-El:

28
    (William) Elliot Dodd (Jr.) (1892-1957), a leading illustrator for *Astounding*. Dodd had 44 full-page drawings and 19 decorations in Harold Brainerd Hersey's *Night* (NY: Privately printed, 1923), a book of poems.
29
    Alastair was the pseudonym of Hans Henning von Voigt (b. 1887), author of *Fifty Drawings* (New York: Alfred A. Knopf, 1925). He also illustrated Walter Pater's *Sebastian Storck* (London, 1927), a copy of which was owned by Donald Wandrei.

Carvings and your letter arrived some days ago. Glad that you and Krang's acolyte[30] were so much taken with the primal and diabolic teraphim. Will write anon. Have recently done a definitive representation of Tsathoggua in serpentine.

   Yrs.,

                    Klarkash-Ton

---

[30] Robert Barlow.

A CLARK ASHTON SMITH BIBLIOGRAPHY AND CHECKLIST

By Glynn Barrass and Edward P. Berglund

INTRODUCTION

Hello and welcome to the second edition of this bibliography of Clark Ashton Smith's works. Since so much of Smith's work has been put back into print since the first edition of this bibliography, it is only proper that it be updated, considering his great contribution to the fantasy and weird fiction genres. We hope you will find it useful and helpful in collecting Clark Ashton Smith's works. If you, the reader, discover any discrepancies or disagreements in the listings, please let us know, and we will gladly acknowledge your help in any future edition.

Glynn - September 1, 2012
Email: batglynn@hotmail.com
Edward - June 15, 2012
Email: eberglund@ec.rr.com

ACKNOWLEDGEMENTS

Glynn: Thank you for updating this bibliography

Edward. You have done a fine job in updating each and every facet of my humble work.

Edward: Many thanks to Glynn for allowing me to update his bibliography, correcting a few items, and restructuring the bibliography somewhat.

WHAT'S IN THIS BIBLIOGRAPHY?

This bibliography (hopefully, once again) contains all published works by Clark Ashton Smith, excluding foreign language editions and single story/poetry appearances in anthologies and periodicals. It also contains non-fiction books written about Clark Ashton Smith, and books inspired by his work and written in tribute to him. A list of the contents for each book is not included, but if you have access to the Internet, you can find the contents for just about every book listed here on The Eldritch Dark website: http://www.eldritchdark.com – without a doubt the best information resource on Clark Ashton Smith on the web or anywhere else in print.

A NOTE ON THE TEXT

The listing convention is as follows: the title is listed alphabetically, followed by the identity of the author or editor, where necessary, then the name of the publisher, then the format of the book – hardcover editions notated by H/C, and paperback and trade paperback editions notated by P/B – then the year of publications, and then information on the book's contents. If a paperback edition is available from the same publisher as the hardcover edition, P/B will follow the H/C notation. Items listed with the C notation are in chapbook format. If a publisher's paperback and hardcover editions are published in different years, there will be a date following the H/C notation and the P/B notation; if published in the same year, the date will follow the P/B notation. Additional dates will denote reprintings by the same publisher, with notation of more than one reprinting in a particular year.

☐ The Abominations of Yondo (Published by Arkham House, H/C, 1960, Short Story Collection)

☐ The Abominations of Yondo (Published by Neville Spearman, H/C, 1972, Short Story Collection)

☐ The Abominations of Yondo (Published by Panther Books, P/B, 1974 [2 printings], Short Story Collection)

☐ The Black Abbot of Puthuum (published by The Ras Press, C, 2007, Short Story)
Terence McVicker mcrarebooks@earthlink.net

☐ The Black Book of Clark Ashton Smith – Edited by Donald Sidney-Fryer and Rah Hoffmann (Published by Arkham House, P/B, 1979, Story and Poetry Collection)

☐ The Black Diamonds – Edited by S.T. Joshi (Published by Hippocampus Press, P/B, 2002, Novel)

☐ The Book of Hyperborea – Edited by Will Murray (Published by Necronomicon Press, P/B, 1996, Short Story Collection)

☐ The Books of Clark Ashton Smith – Edited by Joseph Bell (Published by Soft Books, C, 1987, Bibliography)

☐ The Book of Eibon – Edited by Robert M. Price (Published by Chaosium Books, P/B, 2002, CAS Short Story and CAS-Inspired Short Stories and Poetry Collection)

☐ The City of the Singing Flame – Edited by Donald Sidney-Fryer (Published by Timescape Books, P/B, 1981, Short Story Collection)

☐ Clark Ashton Smith: Artist (Published by Gerry de la Ree, C, 1975, Artwork Collection; distributed through The Hyperborean League amateur press association)

☐ Clark Ashton Smith: Letters to H.P. Lovecraft – Edited by Steve Behrends (Published by Necronomicon Press, C, 1987, Correspondence Collection)

☐ Clark Ashton Smith: Poet (Published by Gerry de la Ree, C, 1975, Poetry and Artwork Collection)

☐ Clark Ashton Smith: The Sorcerer Departs – Edited by Donald Sidney-Fryer (Published by ???, C, 1963, Essays about CAS)

☐ Clark Ashton Smith: The Sorcerer Departs – Edited by Donald Sidney-Fryer (Published by Tsathoggua Press, C, 1997, Essays about CAS)

☐ Clark Ashton Smith: The Sorcerer Departs – Edited by Donald Sidney-Fryer (Published by Silver Key Press,

P/B, 2007, Essays about CAS)

□ A Clark Ashton Smith Bibliography and Checklist – By Glynn Barrass (Published by Black Goat Books, C, 2007, Bibliography)

□ Clark Ashton Smith's Hyperborea – Adapted by Jason Thompson (Published by Mock Man Press, C, 2004, Comic Book of The Tale of Satampra Zeiros)

□ Cycles (Published by Roy A. Squires, C, 1963, Poem)

□ The Complete Poetry and Translations, Volume 1: The Abyss Triumphant – Edited by S.T. Joshi and David E. Schultz (Published by Hippocampus Press, H/C, 2008, Poetry and Translation Collection)

□ The Complete Poetry and Translations, Volume 2: The Wine of Summer – Edited by S.T. Joshi and David E. Schultz (Published by Hippocampus Press, H/C, 2008, Poetry and Translation Collection)

□ The Complete Poetry and Translations, Volume 3: The Flowers of Evil and Others – Edited by S.T. Joshi and David E. Schultz (Published by Hippocampus Press, H/C, 2008, Poetry and Translation Collection)

□ The Dark Chateau and Other Poems (Published by Arkham House, H/C, 1951, Poetry Collection)

□ The Dark Eidolon: The Journal of Smith Studies –
Edited by Steve Behrends (Published by Necronomicon
Press, C, 1989 (# 2), 2003 (# 3), Non-Fiction Magazine
about CAS; retitled from Klarkash-Ton: The Journal of
Smith Studies)

□ The Devil's Notebook: Collected Epigrams and
Pensées of Clark Ashton Smith – Edited by Don Herron
(Published by Starmont House, P/B, 1990, Epigrams and
Pensées Collection)

□ The Door to Saturn: The Collected Fantasies of Clark
Ashton Smith, Volume 2 – Edited by Scott Connors and
Ron Hilger (Published by Night Shade Books, H/C, 2007,
Short Story Collection)

□ The Double Shadow (Published by Wildside Press,
H/C, P/B, 2003, short story collection)

□ The Double Shadow and Other Fantasies (Published by
Auburn Journal Press, C, 1933, Short Story Collection)

□ The Double Shadow and Other Fantasies (Published by
The Strange Company, C, 1978, Short Story Collection)
[distributed through the Esoteric Order of Dagon amateur
press association in Mailing # 21, dated March 1978;
distributed through the Howard Phillips Lovecraft
amateur press association (aka The Necronomicon) in
Mailing # 8, dated September 1979]

□ The Dweller in the Gulf (Published by Necronomicon
Press, C, 1987, 1988, 1993, Short Story; The
Unexpurgated Clark Ashton Smith)

□ The Dweller in the Gulf (Published by The Dweller in the Gulf, C, 1993, Short Story)

□ Ebony and Crystal (Published by Clark Ashton Smith [printed by Auburn Journal Press], H/C, 1922, Poetry Collection)

□ The Emperor of Dreams – Edited by Stephen Jones (Published by Orion Books, P/B, 2002, Short Story Collection)

□ Emperor of Dreams: A Clark Ashton Smith Bibliography – Compiled by Donald Sidney-Fryer and Divers Hands (Published by Donald M. Grant, H/C, 1978, Bibliography)

□ The End of the Story: The Collected Fantasies of Clark Ashton Smith, Volume 1 – Edited by Scott Connor and Ron Hilger (Published by Night Shade Books, H/C, 2007, Short Story Collection)

□ The Fantastic Art of Clark Ashton Smith – By Dennis Rickard (Published by Mirage Press, P/B, 1973, Photographic Collection of CAS's Art)

□ The Fantastic Worlds of Clark Ashton Smith – Edited by James Van Hise (Published by James Van Hise, P/B, 2005, Essays about CAS)

□ The Freedom of Fantastic Things: Selected Criticism on Clark Ashton Smith – Edited by Scott Connors (Published by Hippocampus Press, H/C, P/B, 2006,

Essays on CAS)

□ From the Crypts of Memory (Published by Roy Squires, C, 1973, Prose Poem)

□ The Fugitive Poems of Clark Ashton Smith (First Fascicle): The Tartarus of the Suns (Published by The

□Zothique Edition [Roy A. Squires], C, 1970, Poetry Collection)

□ The Fugitive Poems of Clark Ashton Smith (Second Fascicle): The Palace of Jewels (Published by The Zothique Edition [Roy A. Squires], C, 1970, Poetry Collection)

□ The Fugitive Poems of Clark Ashton Smith (Third Fascicle): In the Ultimate Valleys (Published by The Zothique Edition [Roy A. Squires], C, 1970, Poetry Collection)

□ The Fugitive Poems of Clark Ashton Smith (Fourth Fascicle): To George Sterling: Five Poems (Published by The Zothique Edition [Roy A. Squires], C, 1970, Poetry Collection)

□ The Fugitive Poems of Clark Ashton Smith (First Volume): The Titans of Tartarus (Published by The Xiccarph Edition [Roy A. Squires], C, 1974, Poetry Collection)

□ The Fugitive Poems of Clark Ashton Smith (Second Volume): A Song from Hell (Published by The Xiccarph

Edition [Roy A. Squires], C, 1975, Poetry Collection)

☐ The Fugitive Poems of Clark Ashton Smith (Third Volume): The Potion of Dreams (Published by The Xiccarph Edition [Roy A. Squires], C, 1975, Poetry Collection)

☐ The Fugitive Poems of Clark Ashton Smith (Fourth Volume): The Fanes of Dawn (Published by The Xiccarph Edition [Roy A. Squires], C, 1976, Poetry Collection)

☐ The Fugitive Poems of Clark Ashton Smith (Fifth Volume): Seer of the Cycles (Published by The Xiccarph Edition [Roy A. Squires], C, 1976, Poetry Collection)

☐ The Fugitive Poems of Clark Ashton Smith (Sixth Volume): The Burden of the Suns (Published by The Xiccarph Edition [Roy A. Squires], C, 1977, Poetry Collection)

☐ Genius Loci and Other Tales (Published by Arkham House, H/C, 1948, Short Story Collection)

☐ Genius Loci and Other Tales (Published by Neville Spearman, H/C, 1972, Short Story Collection)

☐ Genius Loci and Other Tales (Published by Panther Books, P/B, 1974, Short Story Collection)

☐ The Ghoul and the Seraph (Published by Gargoyle

Press, C, 1950, Poem)

□ Grotesques and Fantastiques: A Selection of Previously Unpublished Drawings and Poems – Edited by Gerry de la Ree (Published by Gerry de la Ree, C, H/C, 1973, Artwork and Poetry Collection)

□ The Hashish-Eater; or, The Apocalypse of Evil (Published by Necronomicon Press, C, 1989, Poem)

□ The Hashish-Eater; or, The Apocalypse of Evil – Edited by Donald Sidney-Fryer (Published by [Innervisions Group Design Firm], C, 1990, Poem)

□ Hesperian Fall (Published by Clyde Beck, C, 1961, Poem)

□ The Hill of Dionysus (Published by Roy A. Squires, C, 1961, Poem)

□ The Hill of Dionysus – A Selection (Published by Roy A. Squires, H/C, 1962, Poetry Collection)

□ Hyperborea (Published by Ballantine Books, P/B, 1971, Short Story Collection)

□ The Immortals of Mercury (Published by Stellar Publishing Corporation, C, 1932, Short Story)

□ In Memoriam: Clark Ashton Smith – Edited by Jack L. Chalker (Published by The Anthem Series, P/B, 1963, Essays about CAS and Stories and Poems by CAS)

186

☐ Klarkash-Ton: The Journal of Smith Studies – Edited by Robert M. Price (Published by Cryptic Publications, C, 1988 (# 1), Non-Fiction Magazine about CAS, retitled The Dark Eidolon: The Journal of Smith Studies)

☐ Klarkash-Ton and Monstro Libriv (Published by Gerry de la Ree, C, 1974, Poetry and Correspondence Collection)

☐ The Klarkash-Ton Cycle: Clark Ashton Smith's Cthulhu Mythos Fiction – Edited by Robert M. Price (Published by Chaosium Books, P/B, 2008, Short Story Collection)

☐ The Last Continent: New Tales of Zothique – Edited by John Pelan (Published by ShadowLands Press, H/C, 1999, CAS-inspired Short Story Collection)

☐ The Last Heiroglyph: The Collected Fantasies of Clark Ashton Smith, Volume 5 – Edited by Scott Connors and Ron Hilger (Published by Night Shade Books, H/C, 2008, Short Story Collection)

☐ The Last Incantation (Published by Timescape Books, P/B, 1982, Short Story Collection)

☐ The Last Oblivion: Best Fantastic Poems of Clark Ashton Smith – Edited by S.T. Joshi and David E. Schultz (Published by Hippocampus Press, P/B, 2002, Poetry Collection)

☐ The Last of the Great Romantic Poets (Published by Silver Scarab Press, P/B, 1973, Essay on CAS's Poetry)

□ Live from Auburn: The Elder Tapes (Published by Necronomicon Press, C, 1995, Poetry Collection/Cassette)

□ Lost Worlds (Published by Arkham House, H/C, 1944, Short Story Collection)

□ Lost Worlds (Published by Neville Spearman, H/C, 1971, Short Story Collection)

□ Lost Worlds (Published by Bison Books, P/B, 2006, Short Story Collection)

□ Lost Worlds, Volume 1 (Published by Panther Books, P/B, 1974, 1975, Short Story Collection)

□ Lost Worlds, Volume 2 (Published by Panther Books, P/B, 1974, Short Story Collection)

□ Lost Worlds: The Journal of Clark Ashton Smith Studies – Edited by Scott Connors (Published by Seele Brennt Publications, P/B, 2004 (# 1), 2005 (# 2), 2006 (# 3), 2007 (# 4), 2008 (# 5), Non-Fiction Magazine about CAS)

□ Lost Worlds of Space and Time, Volume 1 – Edited by Steve Lines (Published by Rainfall Books, P/B, 2004, CAS-Inspired Fiction and Poetry Collection)

□ Lost Worlds of Space and Time, Volume 2 – Edited by Steve Lines (Published by Rainfall Books, P/B, 2005, CAS-Inspired Fiction and Poetry Collection)

□ The Maker of Gargoyles and Other Stories (Published by Wildside Press, H/C, P/B, 2004, Short Story Collection)

□ The Maze of the Enchanter: The Collected Fantasies of Clark Ashton Smith – Edited by Scott Connors and Ron Hilger (Published by Night Shade Books, H/C, 2009, Short Story Collection)

□ The Miscellaneous Writings of Clark Ashton Smith – Edited by Scott Connors and Ron Hilger (Published by Night Shade Books, H/C. 2011, Short Story Collection)

□ The Monster of the Prophecy – Edited by Donald Sidney-Fryer (Published by Timescape Books, P/B, 1983, Short Story Collection)

□ The Monster of the Prophecy (Published by Necronomicon Press, C, 1988, Short Story; The Unexpurgated Clark Ashton Smith)

□ Moonlight and Other Poems (Published by Dodo Press, P/B, 2009, Poetry Collection)

□ The Mortuary (Published by Roy A. Squires, C, 1971, Prose Poem)

□ Mother of Toads (Published by Necronomicon Press, C, 1987, 1988, 1993, Short Story; The Unexpurgated Clark Ashton Smith)

□ Nero: An Early Poem (Published by Roy A. Squires, C,

190

1964, Poem)

□ Nero and Other Poems (Published by Futile Press, H/C, 1937, Poetry Collection)

□ Nostalgia of the Unknown: The Complete Prose Poetry of Clark Ashton Smith – Edited by Marc and Susan Michaud, Steve Behrends, and S.T. Joshi (Published by Necronomicon Press, P/B, 1988, 1993, Prose Poetry Collection)

□ Odes and Sonnets (Published by The Book Club of California, C, 1918, Poetry Collection)

□ Other Dimensions (Published by Arkham House, H/C, 1970, Short Story Collection)

□ Other Dimensions, Volume 1 (Published by Panther Books, P/B, 1977, Short Story Collection)

□ Other Dimensions, Volume 2 (Published by Panther Books, P/B, 1977, Short Story Collection)

□ Out of Space and Time (Published by Arkham House, H/C, 1942, Short Story Collection)

□ Out of Space and Time (Published by Neville Spearman, H/C, 1971, Short Story Collection)

□ Out of Space and Time (Published by Bison Books, P/B, 2006, Short Story Collection)

□ Out of Space and Time, Volume 1 (Published by

Panther Books, P/B, 1974, Short Story Collection)

□ Out of Space and Time, Volume 2 (Published by Panther Books, P/B, 1974, 1975, Short Story Collection)

□ Out of Space and Time (Published by Bison Books, P/B, 2006, Short Story Collection)

□ Planets and Dimensions: Collected Essays of Clark Ashton Smith – Edited by Charles K. Wolfe (Published by Mirage Press, H/B, P/B, 1973, Essay by CAS)

□ Poems in Prose (Published by Arkham House, H/C, 1965, Prose Poem Collection)

□ Poseidonis (subtitled Tales of Lost Atlantis on cover and spine) (Published by Ballantine Books, P/B, 1973, Short Story Collection)

□ Prince Alcouz and the Magician (Published by Roy A. Squires, C, 1977, Short Story)

□ A Prophecy of Monsters (Published by 13th Hour Books, C, 1996, Short Story)

□ Red World of Polaris: The Adventures of Captain Volmar – Edited by Ronald R. Hilger and Scott Connors (Published by Night Shade Books, H/C, 2003, P/B, 2004, Short Story Collection)

□ A Rendezvous in Averoigne: The Best Fantastic Tales of Clark Ashton Smith (Published by Arkham House, H/C, 1988, 2003, Short Story Collection)

193

□ The Return of the Sorcerer: The Best of Clark Ashton Smith – Edited by Robert Weinberg (Published by Prime Books, P/B, 2006, Short Story Collection)

□ Sadastor (Published by Roy A. Squires, C, 1972, Short Story)

□ Sandalwood (Published by Clark Ashton Smith [printed by Auburn Journal Press], H/C, 1925, Poetry Collection)

□ Selected Letters of Clark Ashton Smith – Edited by David E. Schultz and Scott Connors (Published by Arkham House, H/C, 2003, Correspondence Collection)

□ Selected Poems (Published by Arkham House, H/C, 1971, Poetry Collection)

□ Shadows Seen and Unseen: Poetry from the Shadows: Works of Clark Ashton Smith - Raymond L.F. Johnson with Ardath W. Winterowd (Published by HIH Art Studio, H/C, 2007, About CAS, including a number of poetry facsimiles and one story)

□ The Shadow of the Unattained: The Letters of George Sterling and Clark Ashton Smith – Edited by David E. Schultz and S.T. Joshi (Published by Hippocampus Press, P/B, 2005, Correspondence Collection)

□ Song of the Necromancer: The Poems from Weird Tales – Edited by Stephen Jones (Published by PS Publications, H/C, 2010, Poetry Collection)

□ The Sorcerer's Apprentices: New Tales in the Tradition

of Clark Ashton Smith – Edited by James Ambuehl (Published by Sunken Citadel / Tenoka Press, P/B, 1998, CAS-Inspired Stories, Poetry, and Artwork Collection)

□ Sorceries Gnydron – By Ran Cartwright (Published by Rainfall Books, C, 2011, CAS-Inspired Fiction Collection)

□ Spells and Philtres (Published by Arkham House, H/C, 1958, Poetry Collection)

□ Star Changes: The Science Fiction of Clark Ashton Smith – Edited by Scott Connors and Ron Hilger (Published by Darkside Press, H/C, 2005, Short Story Collection)

□ The Star-Treader and Other Poems (Published by A.M. Robertson, H/C, 1912, Poetry Collection)

□ Strange Shadows: The Uncollected Fiction and Essays of Clark Ashton Smith – Edited by Steve Behrends, Donald Sidney-Fryer, and Rah Hoffmann (Published by Greenwood Press, H/C, 1989, Short Story and Essay Collection)

□ The Sword of Zagan and Other Writings – Edited by Dr. W.C. Farmer (Published by Hippocampus Press, P/B, 2004, Short Story and Poetry Collection)

□ The Tales of Clark Ashton Smith: A Bibliography – By Thomas G.L. Cockcroft (Published by Thomas G.L. Cockcroft, C, 1951, Bibliography)

□ Tales of Science and Sorcery (Published by Arkham House, H/C, 1964, Short Story Collection)

□ Tales of Science and Sorcery (Published by Panther Books, P/B. 1976, Short Story Collection)

□ Tales of Zothique – Edited by Will Murray with Steve Behrends (Published by Necronomicon Press, P/B, 1995, Short Story Collection)

□ Tales of Zothique # 1: In the Latter Days – By Ran Cartwright (Published by Rainfall Books, C, 2007, CAS-Inspired Fiction Collection)

□ Tales of Zothique # 2: The Final Swan Song – By Ran Cartwright (Published by Rainfall Books, C, 2007, CAS-Inspired Fiction Collection)

□ Untold Tales (Crypt of Cthulhu # 27) (Published by Cryptic Publications, C, 1984, Unfinished Stories, Fragments, and Synopses Magazine Collection)

□ The Vaults of Yoh-Vombis (Published by Necronomicon Press, C, 1988 [2 printings], 1993, Short Story; The Unexpurgated Clark Ashton Smith)

□ A Vintage from Atlantis: The Collected Fantasies of Clark Ashton Smith, Volume 3 (Published by Night Shade Books, H/C, 2007, Short Story Collection)

□ The White Sybil by Clark Ashton Smith / The Men of Avalon by David H. Keller, M.D. (Published by Fantasy Publications, C, 1935, Short Story)

□ The White Sybil and Other Stories (Published by Wildside Press, H/C, 2005, P/B, 2006, Short Story Collection)

□ The Witchcraft of Ulua (Published by Necronomicon Press, C, 1988, Short Story; The Unexpurgated Clark Ashton Smith)

□ Xeethra (Published by Necronomicon Press, C, 1988, Short Story; The Unexpurgated Clark Ashton Smith)

□ Xiccarph (Published by Ballantine Books, P/B, 1972, Short Story Collection)

□ Zothique (Published by Ballantine Books, P/B, 1970, Short Story Collection)

BIOGRAPHIES

GLYNN OWEN BARRASS lives in the North East of England and has been writing since late 2006. His work has appeared in over 50 magazines and anthologies including 'Crossed Genres,' 'Lovecraft's Disciples, 'Night Land,' and 'Urban Cthulhu: Nightmare Cities.' He also edits collections for Chaosium's Call of Cthulhu fiction line, and writes RPG material.

Details and news of his latest fiction appearances can be found on his website

'Stranger Aeons: The Domain of Writer Glynn Barrass' www.freewebs.com/batglynn

EDWARD P. BERGLUND is a retired U.S. Marine, and a retired independent paralegal. He has edited The Disciples of Cthulhu (DAW Books, 1976, Chaosium Books, 1996) and The Disciples of Cthulhu II (Chaosium Books 2003), author of Shards of Darkness (Mythos Books, 2000), and compiler of Reader's Guide to the Cthulhu Mythos (2nd ed.) (Silver Scarab Press, 1974). He is currently working on the 3rd edition of RGttCM, his first novel, Shadow Love, and is working with David Sutton in England in bringing out from Shadows Press *Such Things May Be* , a collection of the fiction and poetry of James Wade.

LEIGH BLACKMORE (BCA Writing, Hons) is no stranger to magick, having been a dedicated ritual magician for over 25 years. He first discovered the verse of Clark Ashton Smith, which has been a perennial influence on his own work, at the age of 13. As second President of the Australian Horror Writers Association

(2010-2011), he also edited Midnight Echo Issue 5 and formerly edited Terror Australis magazine. He runs an editorial business, Proof Perfect, and edits SSWFT Amateur Press Association (Sword and Sorcery/Weird Fiction Terminus APA). As critic, editor, poet and story writer, Leigh has twice been nominated for the Ditmar award (for fiction and criticism). Recent essays appear in Studies in the Fantastic and books from Scarecrow Press, and recent poetry in Weird Fiction Review. Leigh's regular reviews appear in US critical journal Dead Reckonings. His verse collection Spores from Sharnoth & Other Madnesses (P'rea Press, 2008, 2010; variant/retitled ed Rainfall Books, 2010) garnered extensive acclaim. Leigh also plays bass in the band The Third Road.

For more info see: http://www.australianhorror.com/member_pages.php?page=86.

RAN CARTWRIGHT Ran has written in a variety of forms and formats for years, from short stories to screenplays. He prefers horror, but has also written science fiction and fantasy satire. Two of his short horror tales were recommended for Bram Stoker awards in 2000. Ran has several horror and fantasy tales in the works, and an episodic road novel. A retired archaeologist, Ran lives in Biloxi, Mississippi with his cat Pixie AKA Madame Lash.

SCOTT CONNORS was recently honoured by the H. P. Lovecraft Film Festival and CthulhuCon for his work in editing the works of Clark Ashton Smith. He has also been twice nominated for the International Horror Guild

Award for his scholarly and critical writings. He was the first scholar to identify Lovecraft's role in the revision of Duane W. Rimel's story "The Tree on the Hill." His most recent book is In the Realm of Mystery and Wonder: The Art and Prose Poems of Clark Ashton Smith (Centipede Press) and is at work on a biography of the Emperor of Dreams. He lives in northern California not far from Clark Ashton Smith's home at Auburn.

MICHAEL FANTINA has had poetry published in North America, the UK and in Australia. His book Alchemy of Dreams, will soon appear from Hippocampus Press.

[It is difficult for me to relate the influence that Smith has had upon me. Whenever or whatever I write he seems not to far away, and has been a constant source of inspiration ever since I discovered him some 38 years ago. My sonnet "The Muse" is directly inspired by Smith's "Absence of the Muse" and my poem "Flame" is directly inspired by his "Ineffability".]

WADE GERMAN: I wrote "Night Vigil for the Necromancer" in response to Smith's last known poem, called "Cycles," which concerns itself with mortality and resurrection in a cosmos governed by laws of eternal recurrence. His poems have appeared in journals and anthologies such as Dreams and Nightmares, Fungi, Hypnos, Nameless, Phantom Drift, Space and Time, Spectral Realms, Strange Sorcery, Weird Fiction Review and A Darke Phantastique (Cycatrix Press), among others. His collection of poems, Dreams from a Black Nebula, is available from Hippocampus Press.

PERRY GRAYSON was born in the American Midwest in the mid 1970s. His family moved to Southern California early on, and it was in SoCal where Perry developed a love for weird and crime fiction. Perry founded Tsathoggua Press in 1994 to publish rare material of interest to fans of H.P. Lovecraft, Clark Ashton Smith and his favourite author, Frank Belknap Long. In addition to Tsathoggua Press, Perry edited and introduced Escape from Tomorrow (1995) by Frank Belknap Long for Necronomicon Press. As a scrivener, Perry has contributed weird fiction material to The Scream Factory, *Crypt of Cthulhu, Other Dimensions* and Necrofile. He was also a staff writer for major newsstand heavy rock and metal mag Metal Maniacs from 1999 to 2009. As a pro musician in the aforementioned heavy rock and metal genres, Perry played guitar from 1997 to 2000 in Destiny's End, writing a majority of material and appearing on two full-length albums released on a large indie label. Tours of the U.S. and Europe ensued. Next, in 2000, Perry took up vocals as well as guitar, founding Artisan with two close friends. Artisan released an EP worth of tunes online in 2003. 2003 also saw Perry teaming up with British pal and axeman Rich Walker from UK metallers Solstice for a multi-national project EP--Isen Torr - *Mighty and Superior.* While still in Artisan, Perry formed his early 1970s style power trio, Falcon with help from his hero and pal Greg Lindstrom (Cirith Ungol). He happily considers Falcon his fondest musical endeavour. Falcon has released two full-lengths thus far. In 2005 Perry played bass guitar on a European tour with doom metal merchants Pale Divine. He now resides in Australia with his wife and three fur babies (cats).

Emptiness" was inspired by adversity faced in the real world in the form of a scumbag slumlord. Clark Ashton Smith's influence is heavy throughout, including one of Perry's fave CAS pieces, "Nada."

CHRISTENE BRITTON-JONES: With CAS's words ringing inside my head I set out not to emulate, but to have fun, and dedicate a few lines of homage to the master of verse, Clark Ashton Smith, with a little hidden assistance from HPL. (Did you notice?)

All of the most memorable writings of his immediately surfaced as I started writing and the rest just flowed; as it usually is wont to do when I write prose.

STEVE LINES is a musician, artist, editor and occasional writer and runs Rainfall Records & Books with John B. Ford and Clive Jones. He has recently released CDs with his bands Stormclouds: *Waiting for Oblivion*; The Doctor's Pond: *Swamp Sickness* and The Ungrateful Dead: *Black Snakes & Rats, Ain't Got No Whiskey* and *The Nightmare Influence* (with John B. Ford, with whom he also wrote the Smith inspired fantasy novel *The Night Eternal* published by Rainfall Books.) He has illustrated books for Hippocampus Press, Centipede Press, Rainfall and others. He plays bass in punk band The Chaos Brothers and guitar in The Doctor's Pond. His story *The Eyes of the Scorpion* was inspired by Smith's Arabian fantasies.

CHARLES LOVECRAFT started writing in 1975, inspired by H. P. Lovecraft. As publisher-editor, he created P'rea Press in 2007 (www.preapress.com) to publish weird and fantastic poetry, non-fiction and bibliography, and to keep traditional poetry forms alive. He has edited nineteen books to now. Charles has seen publication in *Nyctalops*, *Eldritch Tales*, *Fantasy Tales*, *Pablo Lennis*, *Weird Fiction Review*, *Spectral Realms*, *The Poet's Press*, *Black Wings IV*, and *Beyond the Cosmic Threshold*.

ROBERT M. PRICE discovered the Weird Tales Musketeers at the tender age of 13. He is the proud custodian of Clark Ashton Smith's hand-fashioned "Treasure Guardians" (one of them none other than Tsathoggua) bookends, which August Derleth sold to Lin Carter.

WILUM HOPFROG PUGMIRE has been writing weird fiction since 1971. His main genre influences are H. P. Lovecraft, Clark Ashton Smith and Thomas Ligotti. His many books include 'Bohemians of Sesqua Valley' 'The Strange Dark One', 'Gathered Dust & Others', 'Some Unknown Gulf of Night' and 'Uncommon Places,. An omnibus of his work, 'The Tangled Muse' was published by Centipede Press. He is currently writing an entire book inspired by the Life and Works of Oscar Wilde. A champion of the prose-poem, he considers Clark Ashton Smith among the finest writers in that form, and it was Smith's works concerning Medusa that inspired the piece herein. Smith inspires Pugmire to create works of Awful Beauty.

PETE RAWLIK: I found Clark Ashton Smith through Lovecraft, well Derleth really, through the anthology Tales of the Cthulhu Mythos, the stories "The Return of the Sorcerer" and "Ubbo-Sathla". These are two very different stories; one is a traditional occult vengeance story while the other is a fantastical journey through time, but both are wrapped in the trappings of the mythos. Smith's ability to create complex mythologies rife with a sense of antiquity, and comparisons to the works of Tolkien, Cabell and Vance are inevitable and justified. Yet for me, Smith's strength is not in his world-building, but rather in his ability to change styles depending on his subject. It is hard to believe that "Xeethra", "Monsters in the Night", and "Ubbo-Sathla" were written by the same author, but the fact that they were is inspirational, and an example of what writers of weird fiction must strive for. This is why I have tried to root my "Hyperborean Lament" firmly in Smith's tales of that ancient and myth-haunted land, while "Amongst the Stars I Dream" draws inspiration from pieces such as "Medusa of the Skies" and "The Star-Treader." I cannot ever hope to achieve the quality and quantity of work achieved by Smith, but I can dream, and in dreams who knows what can be?

BRIAN M. SAMMONS has penned stories that have appeared in the anthologies: 'Arkham Tales', 'Horrors Beyond', 'Monstrous', 'Dead but Dreaming 2', 'Horror for the Holidays', 'Deepest, Darkest Eden' and others. He has edited the books; 'Cthulhu Unbound 3', 'Undead & Unbound', 'Eldritch Chrome', 'Edge of Sundown', 'Steampunk Cthulhu', 'Dark Rites of Cthulhu', 'Atomic Age Cthulhu', 'World War Cthulhu' and 'Flesh Like Smoke'. He is also the managing editor of Dark Regions Press' Weird Fiction line and continues to write reviews for a number of publications. For more about this guy that neighbours describe as "such a nice, quiet man" you can check out his infrequently updated webpage here: http://brian_sammons.webs.com/ and follow him on Twitter @BrianMSammons

DAVID SCHEMBRI: *The Lord that Reigns Alone*: Smith's fantastic poetry inspired this direction, and his use of the 'Superior Being' theme. I wanted to forge shimmering lights, pondering the question: Can a dim and distant flame—thought to be forgotten—be a raging inferno once again... *The Torturer's Oath*: A recently explored theme by modern contemporaries, which I find refreshing, and also drawing upon the more humorous side of Smith's prose fiction (Checkmate), I wanted to create a union of the two realms. It is intended at the conclusion of this exploration, to be left with a world bathed in viciousness and dark amusement.

This dedication to Clark Ashton Smith is David Schembri's first outing as a poet. He has been published in several print anthologies and magazines.

His has two poems appearing herein, and has placed three poems across Spectral Realms issues 1&2 from Hippocampus Press. David is also the author of the graphic short story collection: 'Unearthly Fables'.

http://davidschembriwriter.yolasite.com/

RICHARD L. TIERNEY: For more than half a century Richard L. Tierney has composed uncompromisingly delicious dark poetry and prose. Born whilst H. P. Lovecraft was still alive, in 1936, he has been one of the foremost Lovecraftian poets of modern times. His books include The Scroll of Thoth (Chaosium, 1997), The Gardens of Lucullus (Sidecar, 2001), and The Drums of Chaos (Mythos Books, 2008). His poetry volumes include Dreams and Damnations (Strange Company, 1975), The Doom Prophet (1976), Collected Poems (Arkham House, 1981), The Blob That Gobbled Abdul (Sidecar, 2002), and Savage Menace and Other Poems of Horror (P'rea Press, 2010).

BRUCE PENNINGTON provided the stunning cover artwork for some of the early Panther paperback editions of Smith's work published in the early 70's, including Lost Worlds 1 and 2, Genius Loci and The Abominations. of Yondo. His work also graced the covers of works by Arthur Machen, H. P. Lovecraft, Frank Belknap Long and August Derleth. In the 70's and 80's he produced hundreds of cover paintings in the genres of horror, science fiction and fantasy, including iconic works for such authors as Frank Herbert, Brian Aldiss, Gene Wolfe, A. E. Van Vogt and Ray Bradbury. In 2011 the Atlantic Bookshop in London hosted an exhibition of his works. Now retired he is currently working on an autobiography to be published by Rainfall Books.

www.ingramcontent.com/pod-product-compliance
Lightning Source LLC
Chambersburg PA
CBHW072234170626
46813CB00003B/1217